M000306549

TANTRA VIDYĀ

TANTRA VIDYĀ

Based on
Archaic Astronomy and Tāntric Yoga

OSCAR MARCEL HINZE

Translation from the Original German by
V. M. BEDEKAR

MOTILAL BANARSIDASS PUBLISHERS
PRIVATE LIMITED • DELHI

First Edition : Delhi, 1979
Reprint : Delhi, 1989, 1997, 2002

ISBN: 81-208-0524-0 (Cloth)
ISBN: 81-208-0560-7 (Paper)

Also available at:

MOTILAL BANARSIDASS

41 U.A. Bungalow Road, Jawahar Nagar, Delhi 110 007
8 Mahalaxmi Chamber, Bhulabhai Desai Rd., Mumbai 400 026
120 Royapettah High Road, Mylapore, Chennai 600 004
Sanas Plaza, Subhash Nagar, Pune 411 002
16 St. Mark's Road, Bangalore 560 001
8 Camac Street, Kolkata 700 017
Ashok Rajpath, Patna 800 004
Chowk, Varanasi 221 001

Printed in India
BY JAINENDRA PRAKASH JAIN AT SHRI JAINENDRA PRESS,
A-45 NARAINA, PHASE-I, NEW DELHI 110 028
AND PUBLISHED BY NARENDRA PRAKASH JAIN FOR
MOTILAL BANARSIDASS PUBLISHERS PRIVATE LIMITED,
BUNGALOW ROAD, DELHI 110 007

PREFACE

It is a great pleasure for me that two of the most important essays out of the work *Tantra Vidyā* (Theseus Verlag Zürich, 1976) have now been translated into English and published in India. I am indebted to the spiritual tradition of India for a number of deep understandings concerning the true nature of man and world. In the years 1974, 1975 and 1976 I had the opportunity to relate some of my discoveries in the field of Tāntric science by delivering lectures in several Indian Universities and, in this way, to give back to my spiritual Fatherland a part of that Tāntric knowledge which was lost for a long time.

In writing these lines, I remember my dialogue in January 1973 with late Swami Pratyagatmananda Saraswati in his hermitage in Calcutta on astronomical aspects of Tantra Vidyā. He, as well as reverend Dr. Gopinath Kaviraj, whom I had met some days before in Varanasi, encouraged me to render the German scripts into English. In this context an amazing event occurred in the same year when I entered the Publishing House Motilal Banarsidass in Delhi for the first time. An old gentleman was sitting in a corner of the office — as it turned out later, he was the then acting Director of Motilal Banarsidass, Mr. Sundarlal Jain — and gazed at me. "What did you write ?" he asked me. "How do you know that I wrote anything at all ?" I asked back. Mr. Jain did not answer my question but repeated : "What did you write ?" Then I showed him some of my papers. Short and to the point Mr. Jain said : "I will publish it".

Some years have passed since that time. Today Mr. N. P. Jain is continuing the work of his grandfather and I am grateful to him for accomplishing now the first publication of Tantra Vidyā in India.

Great efforts have been undertaken by Professor V. M. Bedekar to perform an apt translation of the German original text. He finished this difficult task before he suddenly and very unexpectedly passed away towards the end of the last year.

Now, by going through the English manuscripts I feel that the point has been reached where we have to bring out the treatise just as it is in the present form. Surely the text does not represent an easy reading. But if the reader will actively collaborate with the author, he will, no doubt, gain full insight in this special topic.

OSCAR MARCEL HINZE

Daisendorf/Meersburg
January 26, 1979

CONTENTS

The German word "Gestalt" deserves special attention in this study. As it cannot be translated into English with a proper term, the meaning of the word shall be explained here: "Gestalt" is always the form of a wholeness or totality. Beside this, it includes the meaning of a "bodily" form, even if it is applied to an anorganic form. It points, then, to the liveliness of such an anorganic pattern. If "Gestalt" is applied only to a part of the totality, then it points out that this part has the qualities of an organic member of the whole totality.—As it has become common practice for the term "gestalt psychology" to leave the German word "Gestalt" untranslated, we do the same here also with the terms "Gestalt-Astronomy" and "gestalt-number". In other places the translation of "Gestalt" varies with the context: form, configuration, figure, pattern, shape etc.

UNDERSTANDING ARCHAIC ASTRONOMY

I. On the Psychology of the Archaic Perception

The present investigation is a contribution to the understanding of the archaic astronomy from the standpoint of a psychologist of perception, trained in astronomy. The reason for which this work has been undertaken is the conviction that archaic astronomy has been misunderstood in its essentials by modern researchers in spite of their manifold research into its historical and philological aspects and despite their historical inquiry into art, culture and religion. "Generations after generations of Mesopotamian priests observe from their towers, since the third millennium before Christ, the appearance and the movements in the nocturnal heavens and believe that the movements and changes in the starry world are the revelations of their gods."[1] The *observations* of the phenomena of the heavens, therefore, lie at the basis of the archaic astronomy, that is to say, astrology. From this it follows, in my opinion, that we have to take into consideration certain *laws of the psychology of perception.*

Franz Boll has also felt in a similar way : continuously he has endeavoured to do justice to ancient astrology, because he sought to visualise the psychological situation of that ancient period.[2] He has, thereby, come to the conclusion that astrology has actually to be understood from the artistic standpoint, mainly from the standpoint of the poet. He does not recognize any fundamental difference between the observations of the sky in ancient times and those of the modern times presented in an animated and poetical way. I, however, believe that here a very important point of view had been overlooked and I, therefore, feel it my duty to take up the approaches of Boll concerning the psychological understanding of ancient astronomy and to continue this work in a *methodical* way. Because for any such comprehension, it is, no doubt, absolutely right and even abso-

1 Wilhelm Gundel *Sternglaube, Sternreligion und Sternorakel* (Belief in stars, Religion of Stars and the Oracle of Stars), Heidelberg 1959, p. 62.

2 cf. the book *Kleine Schirften zur Sternkunde des Altertums* (Short articles on the astronomy of antiquity), edited by Victor Stegemann, Leipzig, 1950.

lutely necessary to put oneself—as Boll has done—into the situation of the archaic observers of the heavens. But without considering the knowledge which gestalt psychology, the ethnical psychology and the developmental psychology have placed before us, about the human capacity of perception and about its genesis, the "transposition" of ourselves into the ancient situation would rather lead us to too insufficient or even partially false results.

We shall again consider the citation of Wilhelm Gundel quoted a little while before. He speaks of the observation of the phenomena and movements in the nocturnal sky and we, as scientifically trained Europeans of the 20th century propose uncritically that we would be able to know exactly what the generations of Mesopotamian priests of those times have "seen or observed". Are not over us the same stars today as in those times ? Are not the same movements in the sky going on basically today as then? And from all these, ultimately, do not the same "perceptions" result ?

Without further consideration, one believes that one is entitled to an affirmative reply and thereby to the conclusion that the ancient observer of the sky a few millennia before Christ must have perceived the same phenomena what we, as Western observers of the heavens of the 20th century after Christ, perceive today. The earlier perception is supposed to have been mainly the same as it is today. Only the way of thinking about a particular perception in the earlier times is supposed to distinguish itself from the way in which the *same* perception is thought about today. It is at this point that our critic applies and, unavoidably, brings us to realise that even the daily, spontaneous perceptions of those times must have led to other results than those of the daily observations of today's scientifically cultivated man. I arrived at this comprehension on the basis of certain experiences during my eight years' stay in Java, where I had the occasion to get acquainted with the kind of nature-observation of Sundanese farmers and with their perceptions and thoughts associated with that observation. An intensive study connected with the concrete practices in the field of perception brought me not only the theoretical insight but also the direct experience that the way in which the scientifically trained European of the 20th century perceives, is only *one* among the many possibilities of perception. To put it concretely : One and the same "world of stimuli"[3] does not necessarily lead to one and the same perception.

In order to arrive repeatedly at the same perception in one and the same "world of stimuli", the perceiving person must continuously have one and the same mental *attitude of perception.*[4]

The genetic psychology now shows us that the different possible attitudes of perception together form a single *context* in the sense that they are parts of a uniform development pattern and thereby are produced, one out of the other, in an organic way, and this phylo- as well as ontogenetically. Exactly to the same extent, the corresponding world-concept undergoes change. (For this reason, a modern children's psychologist could name his book[5] about the phases of the mental development of the child as "The development of the children's world-concept"). One could understand this in that way that in the course of development, an always varying light, as it were, falls on the world, whereby certain aspects and perspectives of this world, which had remained unobserved formerly, come forth into view and become relevant, whereas others, on the other hand, recede back in the background. Thus certain dimensions and depths of the world vanish in order to make place for new ones. This stepwisely proceeding change of dominance of the world elements, which follows organic laws, unavoidably, implies a corresponding transposition or new formation of the spontaneous, *objective* world-concept. In order to make clear what is to be understood under a spontaneous objective perception, here are reproduced two figures which are, in general, known under the designation : "geometrical-optical illusions". (See Illustrations 1 and 2).

Everyone can see spontaneously and objectively that both the horizontal lines in Illustraion 1 are slightly bent and, therefore,

3 The idea of "world of stimuli" will be explained in detail later on (see page 5).

4 In the following dissertation, however, I will deliberately not refer to my personal experiences but will refer to that which academic research has brought to light in this field. In doing so, I shall especially have recourse to the work of Heinz Werner, a Stanley Hall Professor of Genetic Psychology at the Clark University in Worcester (U.S.A.).

5 Wilhelm Hansen: *Die Entwicklung des kindlichen Weltbildes* 3rd edition, München 1952.

Illustration 1

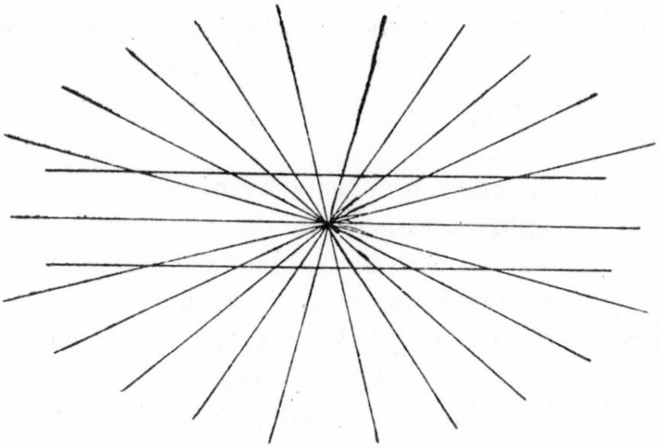

Parallel-illusion according to Hering

are not at all parallel. An unprejudiced spontaneous observation of Illustration 2 accordingly shows that the two circles in the middle are not of equal size. This is the objective result of a spontaneous perception of the diagrammatical illustrations; *objective*, because *everyone* arrives at this result and it is consequently valid *inter-individually*. This result of perception does not change, even though we find out on the basis of *measurement* and *know* on account of this that "in reality" the two lines in question are parallel and the two circles in the middle are of equal size. Accordingly, the *experienced* realit, distinguishes itself clearly from the *physical* reality, which is ascertained as a result of measurement. Today, we are even accustomed to acknowledge only the latter one as *really* true—and, therefore, in the case of both the illustrations, one talks of geometrical-optical *illusions*: The criterion for reality is the physical result of measurement. Physical results of measurement are naturally objective perceptions throughout, as they are verifiable inter-individually. Only, they are *not spontaneous* perceptions. In this way, I would like to separate, conceptually, the objective results of *spontaneous* perceptions from those objective perceptions *carried out through measurements*.

Now, what has been demonstrated in both the illustrations holds good in the whole sphere of our daily perceptions; here as well we can distinguish conceptually the "objective physical"

Illustration 2

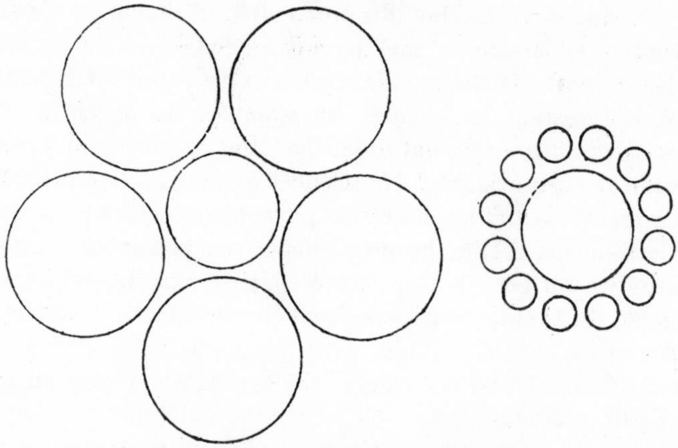

Circle-illusion according to Ebbinghaus

world-concept from the "objective spontaneous" one. And again, another concept is that of the "world of stimuli". This idea stems no doubt from a consideration which looks upon the world from the view-point of physics, but it is not to be equated with the "physical-world-concept". The idea of a "world of stimuli" presupposes the standpoint, which has been selected for methodical reasons that what we call "the world" is nothing else than the sum of all "stimuli" which operate on our senses. This "world of stimuli" in itself is pure chaos. But the physical world-concept represents a mathematical-physical network of arrangements. If, on the other hand, we compare the physical world-concept with the spontaneous world concept, the former looks like one which is fixed and rigid—no doubt, crystal-clear but at the same time a mere sterile skeleton *vis-à-vis* the latter. The direct, spontaneous world-concept is infinitely more many-sided, more "colourful" and more comprehensive than the physical world-concept; it is, above all, full of a pulsating liveliness and "warmth". This is not astonishing if we consider that the physical world-concept is derived *out of* the spontaneous world-concept through a step-by-step elimination of almost all signs which make up our lively world.

The physical arrangement of the world is, therefore, derived from the living reality; but on the other hand, the reverse is not possible. Therefore the physical world-concept is a "derived reality" or, as the phenomenological scientific research calls it, it is a "reduced reality" but it is not at all "the" Reality. Certain dimensions which are in "the" Reality are missing in the physical world-concept. Therefore, the scientist is not supposed, from the point of ideation, to *replace* the spontaneous reality by the physical world-concept, but to let the latter *complete* the former.

Is this not self-evident ? No scientist would wish to replace the living reality by the results of his physical researches—not even in his thoughts ! This, however, happens much more than we realize—we all are, in this respect, highly biased. When, for example, the spontaneous perception shows that the "sun rises", then every educated layman, from the days of his elementary school, "knows" that in "reality" the Sun does not rise, but that the Earth itself is rotating. Or when we see the sun standing on the horizon, so that its lower brim touches it, the modern astronomer knows that "in reality" the sun has just gone down, i.e. it touches the horizon with the *upper* brim. So also every student believes today that the table, on which he works, really consists of innumerable tiniest particles and that between these particles, relatively speaking, there are immense inter-spaces, so that the table, "in reality", consists more of nothing than of something !

These examples demonstrate how the world of direct experience is all too easily *replaced* by the physical world-concept so far as we consider it in thought. And this is everything but scientific because the entire results of the physical researches are only valid under the presupposition of the processes of elimination which have led to these results. Only when these processes of elimination—which imply the stepwise *reduction* of the original reality—emerge into consciousness together with their results, one is able to attribute to these results the grades of reality adequate to them. Because—be it emphasised—the results of physical research are not something "unreal", but they are "real" within the limits which have been set through the kind and extent of methodical elimination by ourselves. That means that the *manner* how we reduce and how science is practised today is not the only possible one. Fundamentally, one could build, under entirely different points of view[6] than those valid today, a

6 The leading points of view, under which science originates, are surely dependent partially on prescientific, cultural-historical and psychological factors.

science—a science which, accordingly, would look different. It is the study of the scientific systems of other people and of other times that teaches us that such other possibilities have actually been realised. We are, however, easily inclined to disqualify such achievements, *a priori*, as "unscientific".

A thorough treatment of this epistemological problem is not possible within the framework of our present essay.[7] But these remarks were absolutely necessary in view of the archaic science of astronomy, which will be discussed in the sequel. Nowadays one holds, in general, to the standpoint that archaic astronomy is, no doubt, fascinating, but, in the ultimate analysis, wrong as it considers the movements in the sky, as they appear to our eyes, to be "real". We are inclined to assume that only we, the men of today, have understood the right thing, that we have finally removed the many errors which were there earlier. To a certain extent, it is even true. But at the same time, the fact that through our scientific presuppositions we have lost something extremely precious not only from the standpoint of a romantic poet who is regretting a fairy-tale like past—even if it was illusionary—but even more so from the exact scientific standpoint, this is what unfortunately today is not generally realised. I hope that after these observations of mine, the reader, when he afterwards will take notice of archaic astronomy in the second part of this essay, will not decide against this old astronomy or, *a priori*, take it to be "wrong", but first regards it as possible that such an astronomy could throughout be a *science*, although that science may have its own characteristic features.

We shall again return to our two diagrammatical illustrations. In illustration 1, if there had been drawn only three horizontal lines, there would not have been the effect of illusion. Only the fact that and the way in which the lines are brought in a wider context, renders this phenomenon possible. The Gestalt-and Holistic-Psychology sees herein—as also in other innumerable phenomena—the manifestation of a law that man primarily first comprehends the whole and only secondarily the parts or members of which the whole is composed. *Thereby, the parts*

7 The publication of a dissertation on this subject is planned under the title: *Methodische Phänomenologie. Skizzen zu einer phänomenologischen Wissenschaftslehre* (Methodological Phenomenology. Sketches on Phenomenological Theory of Science).

may exhibit qualities under the impression of the whole which the parts by themselves do not possess. (Here it may already be anticipated that this proposition applies exactly in the same way for the planets of archaic astronomy. The planets in ancient times were not independent pieces of matter somewhere in empty space but they were organic parts of the archaic sky which maintain their qualities and importance by virtue of their respective position in the whole.) These results of the gestalt psychology now undergo, under the influence of genetic psychology, an interesting extension. For example, from the experimental child-psychology, we learn:

> W. Biemüller and A. Heiss, in their experiments with children and the juveniles of age 3 and upwards, could unanimously demonstrate that in optical experience the form of the totality is the more predominant over the comprehension of individual isolated qualities the further one recedes back in the development (of the child). When Heiss carried out the experiments about geometrical-optical illusions, the result of his experiments was that the younger the children, their estimate of the magnitude of an individual line in a figure was all the more influenced by the experience of the totality and thereby it deviated all the more remarkably from the objective length of the line.[8]

Applied to our figure, it implies as follows: it is undoubtedly the inter-individual and therefore, the objective result of our spontaneous perception that the two horizontal lines are slightly bent, to which *amount*, however, can be different inter-individually. This difference is demonstrably a function of age within a certain period of ontogenetic development. Even in this a rule is ascertained: The earlier in the ontogenetic development, the more do the constituting parts or the individual qualities of a perception shape themselves under the influence of the totality; the later in the ontogenetic development, the more do the individual parts emancipate themselves from the total appearance.

Another result of psychological research may here be added. The earlier in the development, the more affective and emotional the perception; the later in the development, the more do the

8 W. Hansen, *op. cit.* (footnote 5).

perceptions free themselves from their emotional and affective context and become, as they increasingly come under the direction of thought, correspondingly clearer and more matter-of-fact

> "All appearances undergo a development which leads, from the diffused, strongly dynamic and emotional primal states, under suitable conditions to meaningful and clearly organised final forms. This holds good in the perception (F. Sander) as well as in the development of living creatures (F. Krueger, K. Koffka, K. Lewin, H. Werner)."[9]

Quite generally, one can, therefore, inquire into an appearance with regard to its *figural* structure or its emotional or "physiognomic" qualities. The perception can, therefore, be roughly divided into two groups which at the same time correspond to genetic steps: The group of diffuse, emotional primal forms which have only qualities of complexity and exhibit, therefore, no clearly distinguishable parts or substructures. The second is the group of genuine forms which represents a broad spectrum in the beginning of which (joining the first group) the forms are still very diffuse and are filled with emotion and exhibit only indistinct tendencies towards organization. Progressively in the spectrum, the substructures raise themselves from their background and become increasingly more distinct and clear. In the same degree, the exclusive predominance of feeling over perception, i.e. power of the physiognomic expression, is reduced. ("The bad oven looks so darkly at me" exclaims at a certain occasion a small child, thus expressing in a typical way a physiognomic perception of form!) The end of this spectrum is characterized by clear, explicit forms, the pure figural and structural composition of which suits itself in an optimum way for exact mathematical-physical measurements.

Still, a third group can be established, a group which rises above the second group (and, therefore, follows the spectrum of forms). Though the end of the spectrum presents optimum forms whose constituent features stand out distinctly, without losing

9 P. R. Hofstätter, *Psychologie* (Fischer-Lexikon), Frankfurt/Main 1957, p. 151. Compare also: Albert Wellek *Ganzheitspsychologie und Strukturtheorie* (Holistic Psychology and Structure Theory), Bern 1955, pp. 62-68.

their embedding in—or relation to—the totality. The next step beyond the spectrum already takes us into the sphere of *isolation* and *partition*, i.e. *atomization*—in the sphere, where the parts stand out and have become independent to such a degree that the connection with the original whole has been lost.

To summarize, it can be said, in general, in the case of the perception of forms that every form can be investigated:

a) in its pure figural constitution,
b) in its physiognomic aspect or its content of expression,
c) related to a), the constituent parts or the elements of the total form can be taken out of their connection with the whole through measurement, and can be investigated separately.

It would now appear possible that in particular cases, the forms are not recognized as totalities and that instead of the latter, a heap of isolated details is perceived. Where this occurs, the results of possible measurements, afterwards, are no more traced back to an already previously perceived formed totality as such, but are arranged according to some scientific viewpoints and synthesized into a constituent part of the physical world-concept. Basically, today's astronomy represents one such theoretical synthesis from the point of the archaic astronomy.

I will soon demonstrate the phenomenon of the *partition* by giving an example. But before that, I would like to add something to supplement the idea of "Gestalt". The geometrical figures are examples of "spatial" forms and are also named as *simultaneous forms* (Simultan-Gestalten). Also, a tree, a chair and a painting are simultaneous forms, the chief characteristic of which is that they spread themselves out in *space*. But there is also another kind of form (Gestalt): the temporal or *successive form* (Sukzessiv-Gestalt). To this belong e.g. the melodies, the spoken words. These forms spread themselves out in time; they unfold themselves in the time-dimension. We generally understand a plant as a simultaneous form. But this is only *one* aspect of the plant; in no smaller measure, it is also a successive form, a temporal wholeness, if we take into consideration its whole development with the phases of its rise and disappearance. From this standpoint, the "spatial" form "plant", which we survey at a glance, is only a part of the whole temporal form, only a simultaneous "accord" whose individual tones represent the parts of the plant, spatially differentiated, in the "melody" of the total plant-form. The plants and all living beings are forms in the space-time-continuum; they are spatial-temporal wholes.

In the course of the history of mankind, we have been continually losing the sense for the temporal. In its place, we have developed in an increasing measure a sense for the spatial. Characteristic in this connection, as one reads in the works of Hans Kayser, is the loss of the "world-listening" (akroasis) in favour of the "world-view". As a matter of fact, the *ear* is, above all, meant for the comprehension of the *temporal* appearances, while the *eye* is meant for the perception of the *spatial* appearances. If we investigate deeper the nature of the temporal formation of configurations, it becomes necessary to introduce an idea which has been defined for the first time by the great Hamburg psychologist William Stern: the idea of the *presence-time*. This idea is so essential for us that I would best quote the words of its author:[10]

"In the case of time, the problem of perception is put somewhat different from that of space. Because, the perception is directed to that which is present; but so long as man regarded the present in a mathematical way as point of time, it was impossible to press into this "point" the experience of a succession or a duration. One then had to help oneself with something like the following: In the later *point* of time, the earlier perception has still an after-effect as an idea which can be related to or compared with the just occurring perception.

Now there are certain temporal experiences of this kind, e.g. in watching of movements. When I observed many times the hour-hand of a watch, it shows at every isolated act of perception an apparent position of rest. But in the second act of perception, I can remember the earlier different position and draw therefrom the following conclusion: The hour-hand has moved during the interval. Hereby, the occurrence of time is, therefore, experienced only in terms of idea or thought. But is this a unique way of experience ? Would I be able to comprehend

10 William Stern: *Allgemeine Psychologie auf personalistischer Grundlage* (General Psychology on the foundations of personality), Den Haag, 1950, 8th chapter I.3 'About the Temporal Perception.'

the coincidence of a perception with a recollection, as it is given to me in the second act of observation, as a sign at all for a temporal occurrence lying *between*, if such an occurrence would not be known to me out of much more direct experience ?

I take into consideration now the second-hand of a clock and have an entirely different experience. I *see* that it moves, see it with the same clearness as I see its colour and its size. Another example: I hear the word "trālala". Then to me is present the succession of the three syllables and of the dactylic rhythm in unitary and direct perception; then it is present *as* a series and a temporal pattern. It is not that the impression of the first two syllables creeps into the third, so that in the last point of time, I had the "perception" of the third and at the same time the idea of both the first syllables. This "last *point* of time" does not in any way have an isolated existence for my perception, because the latter embraces the whole *stretch* of time.

There are, therefore, perceptions which, without losing their unity and clarity, fill out a certain span of time and can have the temporal content of this span as object. This span of time, inside which a direct perception of time is possible, is designated by me as *presence-time*.

The paradox which appears to attach itself to this "extended present" is today overcome through the fact that we can no more regard the mathematical consideration as authoritative for our personal life. (....):

The psychical presence-time is constricted; that is why I am not able to comprehend the change in position of the hour-hand in one single act of viewing and am thrown back here on comparison and thought.

If I beat a three-measure in the movement of Waltz-dance, I hear a rhythm; if on the other hand, I allow three seconds to lapse between every two tones of beats, the experience of the rhythm is completely lost; I make three separate perceptions which are, no doubt, referable to one another but which cannot structure or arrange themselves any more for the direct experience of a rhythmical temporal pattern.

Now, in this last case, we have a distinct example of partition and atomization. The three tonal beats have likewise fallen out of the whole and have isolated themselves into three separate perceptions.

After what has been said above, it would be significant to refer to the so-called "Phi-phenomenon" of Wertheimer:

> When we project onto a screen a vertical line A, make it to disappear again and let it be followed by a horizontal line B, likewise projected, there will arise, if the time-interval between the two projections is about 1/5 of a second, the successive impression of "first A then B". In a time-interval of about 1/50 of a second, both the lines appear simultaneous and form, therefore, a right angle (a simultaneous impression). During a time-interval of about 1/16 second, there arises the impression that the line A tilts towards the horizontal position B: there arises the phenomenon of a *single* line, moving itself. "Not rarely it is perceived, how the movement continuously strikes over the space between the beginning and end positions (Field-completion)".[11]

This phenomenon is not derivable from the properties of its parts (the parts are : a vertical line, a horizontal line, and a time-interval of 1/16 second) by which the basic thesis of the gestalt and holistic psychology becomes pronounced: While the totality (which is here the line "moving itself") *needs* the parts, the "atoms" (which are here : the two lines and the definite time-interval), in order to appear as such, it is itself always more than, and even in its essence something *different*, from the sum of its parts.

Further, the time-interval of 1/16 second is evidently to be regarded as the presence-time of this phenomenon of movement. We shall again add here a result of genetic psychology : It deals with the experiments of the researchers Meili and Tobler:[12]

11 Hofstätter, *op. cit.* p. 145 (see above footnote 9).

12 Described in: Heinz Werner, *Comparative Psychology of Mental Development*, New York, Chicago, Los Angeles, 1948, p. 68.

> Some experiments have shown that the optical field of the child is dynamic to a far greater degree than that of the adult. These two investigators (Meili and Tobler) compared the ability of 38 children five to twelve years of age to see apparent movement with the corresponding ability in 22 adults. It was demonstrated that the children could discern movements in the kinematographically projected visual forms at a lower rate of succession than could the adults. Children between the ages of twelve and fourteen represented a mean between the greater faculty in younger children and the lesser in adults.

What does this experiment show other than the fact that the presence-time with the younger ones is *longer* than in the case of the grown-ups and that it evidently decreases with increasing age ? We have here something like the temporal "pendant" to the results described earlier (p. 8) of W. Biemüller and A. Heiss, "that in optical experience, the totality predominates the more over the perception of individual qualities the further back in the development." Similarly, we could formulate the results by Meili and Tobler with reference to the Phi-phenomenon: namely that during the temporal succession of two projected lines, the totality—the uniform movement of a *single* line—is perceived the more distinctly the further back in the development, i.e. the younger the child. These two "optical illusions" are certainly not entirely congruent—the one in a purely spatial sphere, e.g. the illusion of the parallels and the other in a spatio-temporal sphere, e.g. the Phi-phenomenon. The similarity of these cases lies, nevertheless, in the predominance of the totality over its parts as a *function of age.*

It is in the same age of a child that the estimation of the size of the individual lines of a geometrical-optical figure is more strongly influenced by the experience of the totality than in a higher age. During a certain temporal succession of projected lines, the child perceives a uniform movement, where a higher age sees only separate parts (two spatially and temporally separated lines).

A greater or lesser presence-time is evidently the expression for the greater or lesser capacity to perceive successive appearances as a whole. When, for example, a melody is played on the piano, the capacity to listen to this melody as a whole depends on the fact that the time-interval between every two tones lies inside the acoustic presence-time. If this interval is too long—i.e. if the piece is played much too slowly, then the experience of the melody gets lost and we hear only a series of isolated tones separated through pauses (partition).

One could imagine an extreme case in which two groups of men sit in a hall, in which a piece of music is presented for listening. One group has an acoustic presence-time which allows its possessors to hear the musical piece as such—as a uniform melody. The other group may, on the other hand, have so short a presence-time that they hear only isolated tones. While the listeners of the first group will be fully absorbed in the experience of music, those of the second group, of course, will be bored. What is it that "objectively exists" in this case ? Is it what the first group listens to (i.e. the melody) or is it what the second group hears (an unconnected sequence of tones) ? Undoubtedly both groups make objective perceptions—only it is equally doubtless that the first group has a *more comprehensive* perception, out of which the perception of the second group can be derived through a corresponding reduction. In other words, the data of perception of the second group are contained in those of the first group; on the other hand the reverse is not true. We could now imagine that in the second group, there are some physicists, who, angry with the strange behaviour of the persons of the first group (who enjoy the music), introduce an exact research for the "naked facts": every little tone is investigated. The amplitudes and frequencies are determined exactly and numerically, as also the interval of time between the individual tones. All this can be made very exactly, with extreme precision; still in spite of it all, one will never be able to comprehend in this way the *musical whole* intended by the composer. Naturally, no physicist of today will seriously doubt in this connection; the example was chosen with intention as too transparent. Every physicist will, for example, fully acknowledge the possibility of a musical science, which definitely presupposes the whole musical experience. But we shall see later on, when we come to speak on the Gestalt-Astronomy, how this very example applies[13] also the present-day scientist in a modified but still analogous form.

13 In spite of what has been said, there are physicists who think as follows:

Before clearly expressing the significance of the results gained heretofore for the understanding of archaic astronomy, let us consider a few additional points. We have seen how the perception in the case of men growing in age, goes through certain regularly definable changes. The results of the general developmental psychology demonstrate that the laws of change found, have in general genetic significance, and that formally the basic laws of children's perception are valid for the perception of the people who, today, still live in a natural state. Therefore the perception of a child in its formal structure may throw light on the way of perception of mankind in the past epochs.[14]

Thus there is, for example, an agreement between the memory of today's child of modern civilization and the memory of today's adult in a natural state. However different, the modern child and the archaic natural man may be, there are still "genetic parallels" (as William Stern puts it) which show that the adult natural man represents the same genetic step as that of the modern child of a certain age-group. To this step may correspond an early step of a certain people of ancient past times.[15]

Thus one can start from the assumption that the increase of the presence-time while going back further in development of young men, also holds good for mankind as a whole; that, for example, people who lived a thousand years before Christ, had in general a greater presence-time than the grown-up cultured persons of today. But this does not concern the presence-time *as such*, which is only an expression for a more or less integrating perception of successive forms, but it generally concerns the

Ultimately *real* would be only such certain items which are expressible in frequencies and amplitudes, which one is accustomed to name as tones; there would not exist a "musical piece", this would just be a designation for a subjectively conditioned "psychic reaction", occurring "inside" ourselves only, as a result of the physical vibrations produced in the external world. The scientific untenability of such a way of thinking cannot be dealt with here. It will receive an exhaustive treatment in another place.

14 In order to preclude misunderstandings it must be again emphasised that it implies a purely *formal* resemblance. When, for example, we call an old man "childish" we do not positively consider that he is throughout like a child; only in a purely formal aspect he does exhibit the ways of behaviour which otherwise only occur among children and are normal in their case, so that it, therefore, deals in this case, with the case of a morbid conformity.

15 Compare Heinz Werner: *Einführung in die Entwicklungspsychologie*, (Introduction to developmental psychology), Munich 1959, p. 18.

particular capacity of a certain genetic level to perceive a totality where a higher degree in the genetic scale allows only to perceive a heap of unconnected particulars. But this latter step again renders possible the simultaneous perception of totalities in cases in which a next higher degree allows to perceive only the isolated elements and so on. When, for example, Thurnwald[16] says that "the Mėlanese of Bismarck-Archipelago, when talking about *ciki* (drops) think simultaneously not only of a drop of water which falls from a tree but also of a lot more, e.g. of the moist spots which it leaves behind, or of the noise of the falling drops, or of the regular intervals at which drops fall from the roof, and, finally, they also think of the unexpected sudden fall of the drop itself." Thus we see how in this case, the natural man spontaneously comprehends, as parts of a whole, elements which are, according to us, isolated: 1) the drop itself, 2) the moist spot, 3) the noise of falling drops, 4) the regular interval, etc. Also the phenomena like the extraordinary capacity of memory which is found among natural men point out a greater "presence" for things which a modern civilized man cannot comprehend directly. Thus, for example, Galton reports "about the fabulous geographical memory of an Eskimo whom Captain Hall had observed. This man drew out of his memory a map of a region through which he had passed once or twice with his canoe. The straight distance across the region was about 1100 English miles while the distance along the coastline was at least six times as great. The comparison of this rough drawing of the Eskimo with the map of the Admiralty of 1870 showed a remarkable agreement. Galton has never seen, among the many land-maps of the white men one such map which had been drawn out of memory and which could stand comparison with the map of the primitive Eskimo."[17] Or another example: "W. E. Roth relates about the indigenous inhabitants of North-West Queensland that they possessed the capacity to reproduce most precisely the text of a series of songs, even though the text was unintelligible to them, and it took five nights time to sing those songs fully."[18] Werner also adds the reports of Thilenius about the capacity of

16 cf. Werner, *op. cit.* p. 12.
17 Werner, *op. cit.* p. 104.
18 *ibid.*

the folks of the South Sea islands, to reproduce the songs as well as the endlessly long line of their ancestors, without any external aid. "We find here" remarks Werner in conclusion, "everywhere a power of memory which is so strong that it, in its sensuousness, already reminds one of a process of perception."[19]

This last conclusion is very important. It is concerned with an additional property of the earlier stages of development: the further one recedes back in the stages of development, the tighter perception and imagination are still connected with one another; the later in the development, the more they differentiate themselves from one another. "This lesser differentiation is shown by the fact that the perceptions possess much more the character of idea and the ideas possess much more the character of perception than in the case of the elevated Europeans."[20]

It is necessary in this place to describe, in short, the phenomenon of "*eidetic images*".[21] An eidetically gifted person (mostly to be found among *children*; adult eidetics are most often found among artists) can, for example, recall a picture seen before and can project it in any place in his surroundings. The eidetic then sees the picture in such clearness and sensuous freshness that it, in this respect, does not differ from a real, optical perception. In such eidetic images, certain details can be perceived *afterwards* and can be exactly described, details which were not noticed in the original. The perceptional quality of these images is so high that, for example, the eidetic image of a cupboard, which is projected in some place, really covers all the objects *behind* the cupboard, as if in that place, there stood a real tangible cupboard.

The eidetic image has one thing in common with *imagination*, namely that it has no real localization in the external tangible environment and that it is perceived by the eidetic as "subjective" i.e. he knows that he has himself brought forth the eidetic image and that it does not really exist as perceptible in his environment (in contrast to the hallucinations of the mentally ill). This capacity, as said before, is found rather often among children, especially of the age-group 8 to 12 years, and disappears mostly again at the onset of puberty. Werner connects the previously

19 *ibid.*

20 *op. cit.* p. 105.

21 The existence of these images was discovered by the Scholar Urbantschitsch and was closer investigated by the brothers Erich and Walter Jaensch.

mentioned extraordinary capacity of memory with natural men with the phenomenon of the eidetic talent.

One can briefly characterize the eidetic images by saying that the qualities of perception as well as of imagination reconcile themselves in it. But now the perceptions of natural men, as can be demonstrated, have in a much higher degree the character of imagination than those among civilized Europeans, whereas in the reverse, "the world of ideas of primitive men contains in their sensuous freshness features which otherwise occur only to the perceptions of the average civilized men. The subjective images are richer in eidetic appearances; they stand decidedly closer to those eidetic images which Jaensch has found typical for the children's world, than what the case is among the civilized Europeans."[22] The eidetic images are today most frequently met with in the optical sphere, without, however, exclusively restricting themselves to it. (Remark the optical sphere of the word "image" in this connection; also the Greek word "eidos" means "image" or "view"). There are also acoustic "eidetic images" and, still more rarely, also the "eidetic images" of smell and taste. On the other hand, the tactile-motor "eidetic images" are again less rare.

In conclusion, another genetic law can be formulated as follows: The further one recedes back in the development, the more the individual areas of sense, which in the culture-men of today are clearly differentiated from one another, are found still united with one another. This is a phenomenon which is indicated by the word "synaesthesis" ("sympathy"). One speaks of a synaesthesis, when one for example reacts to an acoustic stimulus not only with the ears but also with the sensations of sight or with the sensations of other areas of sense. The earlier the stage of development, the stronger and more comprehensively the sensuous perception of the area of one organ brings, along with it, corresponding perceptions of other areas of sense, even movements in the motor activity. For example, the *sight* of certain colours and forms leads to definite impulses of movement, which are noticed no more as such by the culture-men of today, but which, in earlier stages of development, find expression in *external* gestures and movements. Through experiments with drugs (mescalin), in which the persons under experiment are artificially thrown back

22 Werner, *op. cit.* p. 105.

into archaic stages, one can impressively demonstrate the increasing disappearance of the limits between separate areas of senses as well as between thought, feeling and action, between the inner and the outer world, etc. A person under experiment of Beringer communicates the intoxication of mescalin thus: "I felt, saw, tasted, smelt the sound. I was myself the sound. It was a similar thing when I thought of my hands and feet. I thought, saw, felt, tasted my hands...."[23]

In mental illnesses also, a similar regression is found as is shown by the utterance of a sick person described by P. Schilder: "When I say 'red', it is an idea which can be expressed in colour, music, feeling, thought and disposition. When this idea is produced in some way, then one simultaneously experiences all the other forms of the idea as well. One has therefore *not five senses but only one...*"[24]

Naturally, such a sort of experience is not by itself morbid, it was normal in earlier phases of mankind. But today there are only a few rare individuals who, on account of their special constitution, are capable of such experiences to a certain degree. However, in a superficial form, the synaesthesis is today relatively common (according to Remplein, upto about 12% of the population).[25] One sees for example, colours and forms while hearing ringing sounds. The synaesthesis becomes manifest in the language when one speaks of "screaming", "cold" and "warm" colours, "rude" or "rough" sounds or clamour and of "a dark" voice, etc.

We now can realize the significance of the above described phenomena with regard to the archaic astronomy. The question which confronts us is this: How must the starry sky have appeared to the ancient observer ? It is interesting to find that the answer to be given to this question and to be substantiated with the help of the psychology of perception, had been already anticipated by two researchers—Julius Schwabe and Hermann von Baravalle. The answer of these researchers did *not* originate from psychology but was arrived at solely on the ground of their own fields of

23 Werner *op. cit.*, p. 66

24 Werner, *op. cit.*, p. 65.

25 H. Remplein, *Psychologie der Persönlichkeit* (Psychology [of Personality) Munich/Basle, 1963, p. 313.

research. Julius Schwabe writes: "To us the ball which is thrown is a concrete, visible, seizable thing; the parabola of its course is something abstract, a mere thought. This difference seems to have been unknown to pre-historic man. The yearly circular path of the sun was to him as objective and concrete as the sun itself. The corresponding thing holds good for all the other geometrical symbolic figures, developed out of the Zodiac. In their linear structure, which we call ideational or abstract, the pre-historic man saw, so to speak, the strong beam-frame of the cosmic edifice."[26]

In his textbook,[27] Hermann von Baravalle notes: "Today we possess no direct capacity of perception of rhythmical processes which accomplish themselves within such a long period. [What is meant here is the movement of the stars.] That such a capacity for perception should not have existed in earlier millennia, either, would be an unproved assumption. We observe in various fields a change in human capacities. They show the tendency to turn more and more towards speedier proceses. The astronomical conditions show, however, as a characteristic the fact that they lie, through their slowness, under the threshold of processes, from which we can still today receive direct impressions."

The question which requires to be handled, is how the sky looked to the archaic observers who carried out continuously the observations through years and decades of years, with minimum technical instruments but with maximum effort of all their perceptional abilities. We must think that the ancient observers of the sky must have been equipped with an extraordinarily vital perceiving memory, with the *capacity to view together the phenomena in connection with one another to a presentic unity, phenomena which, today for us, lie temporally too much apart to be still perceived as belonging together.* We must not, at the same time, forget the other essential feature characterizing the ancient observer of the heavens. This feature is: That on one hand, the different areas of perception which to us are already widely differentiated apart from each other, and on the other hand, the

26 Julius Schwabe, *Archetyp und Tierkreis,* (Archetype and Zodiac) Basle, 1951, p. XXIII.

27 H. v. Baravalle, *Die Erscheinungen am Sternenhimmel* (The Phenomena in the starry heavens), *Lehrbuch der Astronomie zum Selbststudium und für den Unterricht,* Dresden 1937, p. 133.

areas of imagination and recollection still formed a unity to a high degree. This evinced, among other things, that the recollections gained the character of sensuous perception. We are today too much inclined to consider everything out of *our own* sphere of experience and, therefore, do not easily arrive at an approximately adequate idea of the totally different sort of experience of mankind in earlier stages.

Therefore, I request my readers to realize the liveliest possible by all means of their imagination what has been said above. Let us imagine that we are observing the phenomena of the sky every day or every night, respectively. We would then, for example, see in one night the planet Mars, having its place between many fixed stars. In the next night, we would see it again, and again in the following night, and so on. Now, the modern observer of the sky would remember after some weeks that Mars first stood "there", in a particular position, then somewhat further to the left, etc. In short, he would remember the isolated "positions" of Mars (certainly not without the help of a map, prepared for this purpose, of the corresponding regions of the sky on which he would mark, e.g. with points, the successive positions of Mars). The archaic observer of the sky, on the other hand, recollecting back in the course of the weeks, would not perceive the isolated positions of Mars, but he would rather perceive a *definite, characteristic, serpentine movement* of Mars between the fixed stars, as to him in every following night the preceding positions of Mars are still present in fresh liveliness. (The character of *perception* of such "recollecting" back requires to be especially emphasised). Thereby the *form*, as also the continuous *changes of velocity* of this movement strikes our attention spontaneously and strikingly. If we add—if possible the simultaneous—observation of the movements of Jupiter and Saturn, then there comes strikingly into view the characteristically relatively *quicker* movement of Mars as compared with Jupiter and Saturn. But not less impressive is the way in which Jupiter and Saturn also stand out in relation to Mars, as also in relation to one another, in respect of the kind and velocity of their movements. Jupiter and Saturn thus show also their pronounced and significant character. We shall speak later in the second part of our dissertation somewhat more exhaustively about the movement of these three planets, especially of Mars.

It can now be understood why the Babylonians characterized the phenomena of the heavens as "Sitir Same", as "a script of the sky", how also such a script of the sky must have led straightway to a *graphology of the phenomena of the sky*. The proof that one such "graphology" has been, as a matter of fact, carried out, even according to the same basic rules which have been developed by today's graphology, remains reserved for a later work.

The name Gestalt-Astronomy appears to me suitable to designate such a science which comprehends the individual elements of the sky, especially the planets, as constituents of successively appearing unitary forms. Evidently, the archaic knowledge of the sky was an astronomy of such unitary successive forms. As will be clear from the second part of this dissertation, here we deal with not only the configurations of the already described movements of Mars, Jupiter and Saturn, which are continuously going on, but also with a class of forms of a different kind with which I would not deal now. Seen as a whole, this dissertation represents only a part of the wide field of Gestalt-Astronomy: namely a section out of the chapter on the *configurative Gestalt-Astronomy*. Man in ancient times has not only perceived the configurations in the sky as such, but has also *interpreted them physiognomically*. We can accordingly designate this aspect of the archaic knowledge of the sky as *physiognomical Gestalt-Astronomy* in which the graphology of the sky, mentioned earlier, has its place. Finally, the archaic priests who watched the heavens, comprehended, at the highest stage of their graphological interpretation of the sky, the stars and their movements as cosmic *symbols* which, according to a corresponding interpretation, provide explanation about the most essential questions of human life, about the questions of the conduct of life, of the social order, and of the life beyond. In short, all these questions embracing the total political-social as also the ethical-philosophical-religious aspects of life got their answer on the basis of a systematic interpretation of the symbols of the heavens. Thus the configurative and physiognomical Gestalt-Astronomy culminated in a science which we can designate as the *symbolical Gestalt-Astronomy*.

This highest form of the ancient knowledge of the heavens cannot be described in the following second part of this dissertation. But while we shall demonstrate the configurative Gestalt-Astronomy in the context of the Kuṇḍalinī-Yoga system and shall therethrough give simultaneously for the first time a clarification from the point of Gestalt-Astronomy of the "lotus-flowers", of their sequential series and the number of their petals, a plane will be at least implicitly prepared through the special selection of the demonstration-material—the plane on which the symbolical Gestalt-Astronomy is operating.

II. The Seven Lotus-flowers of the Kuṇḍalinī-Yoga as a Representation of Archaic Gestalt-Astronomy

(*i*) An Introductory Elucidation of the Illustrations of Avalon

Concerning Kuṇḍalinī-Yoga

The comprehensive presentation which deals with this theme is the fundamental work, even today unsurpassed, of Arthur Avalon (the pseudonym of Sir John Woodroffe) viz. *The Serpent Power* (New edition, Madras 1958; first edition 1918). This book holds good also in India as a work of the first rank. It contains the translation of two works from Sanskrit: 1) *Ṣaṭ-cakra-nirūpaṇa* ("Description of and Investigation into the six Bodily Centres") and 2) *Pādukā-Pañcaka* ("The Fivefold Footstool").

The *Ṣaṭ-cakra-nirūpaṇa* was composed in the year 1577 by Śrī-Pūrṇānandayati, a famous Tāntrika Sādhaka from Bengal, and commented upon by the Tāntrika Kālīcaraṇa. Avalon adds to this translation an Introduction and also an exhaustive commentary. The illustrations 3a to 9 in the present work are the reproductions[28] of the corresponding illustrations in Avalon's work and concern the text of the Ṣaṭ-cakra-nirūpaṇa. Only the illustration of the seventh centre is left out because it hardly shows more than illustrations 3a.

The Centres

In the Yoga, especially in the so-called Kuṇḍalinī-Yoga, called also Laya-Yoga, the symbolic idea of *cakra* (wheel, circle) or *padma* (lotus) plays a central role. For the Yogi the "lotus-flowers" are real existing centres, which are even localizable in definite places of his body. Seven of them are regarded as the most important ones. (See Illustrations 3a and 3b).

28 The illustrations originate from the book by Werner Bohm, *Chakras Lebenskräfte und Bewusstseinszentren im Menschen* (O. W. Barth Publication, München-Planegg 1953).

Illustration 3a

Localization of the seven "Lotus-Flowers" in the human body according to the system of the Kuṇḍalinī-Yoga (for schematic representation see illustration 3 b)

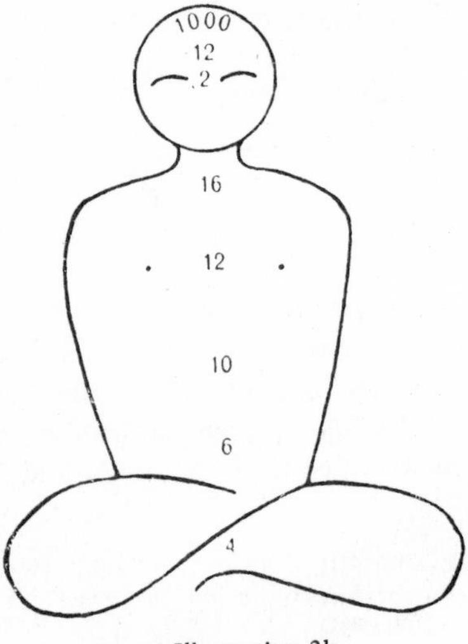

Illustration 3b

Schematic representation of the localization of the seven "Lotus-Flowers" in the human body

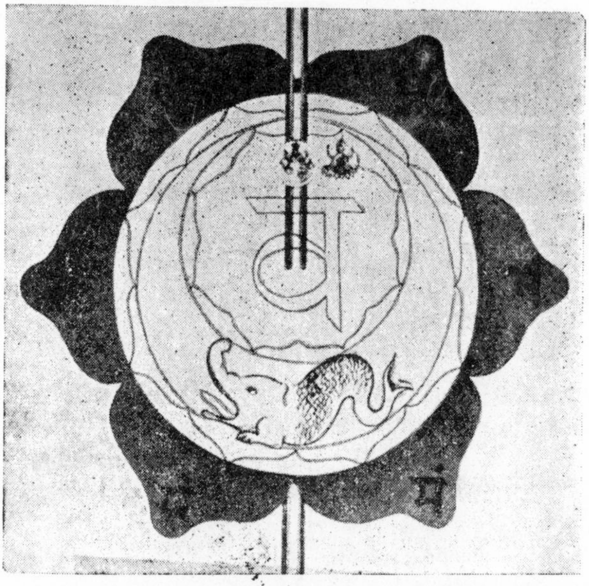

Illustration 4
2nd centre: Svādhiṣṭhāna-Cakra wih 6 petals. 3 labials and 3 semi-vowels

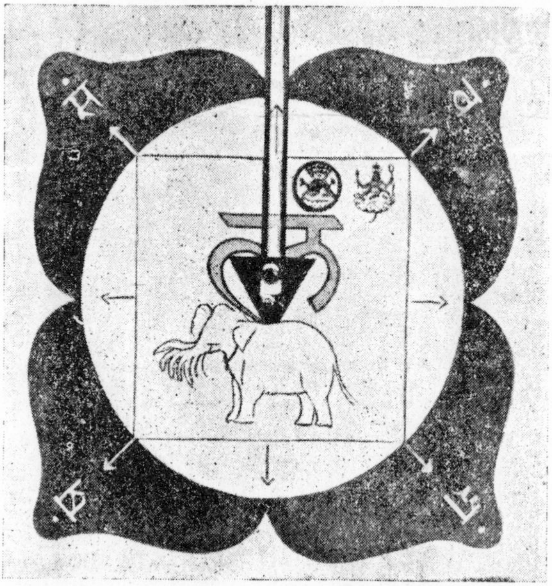

Illustration 5
1st centre: Mūlādhāra-Cakra with 4 petals. 1 semi- vowel and 3 sibilants

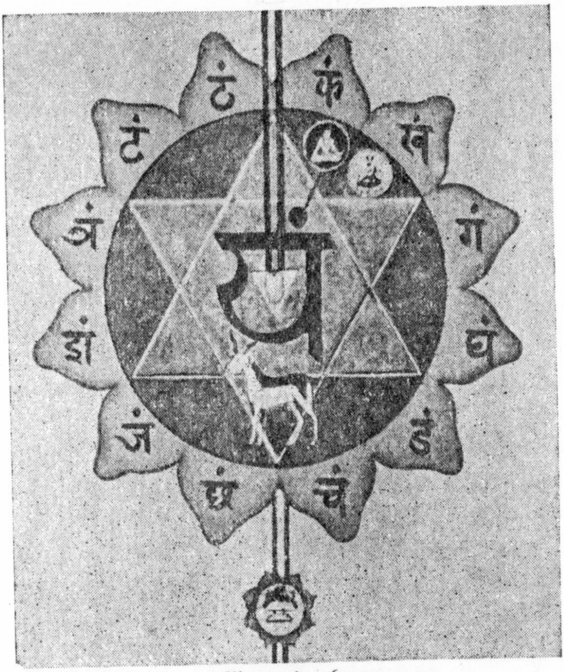

Illustration 6

4th centre: Anāhata-Cakra with 12 petals. 5 gutturals, 5 palatals and 2 cerebrals

Illustration 7

3rd centre: Maṇipūra-Cakra with 10 petals. 3 cerebrals, 5 dentals and 2 labials

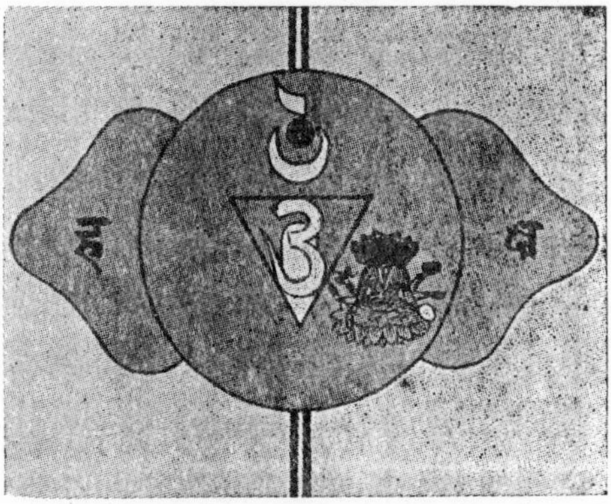

Illustration 8
Ājñā-Cakra with 2 petals. The right petal Ha is connected with the *Sun*; the left petal is connected with the *Moon*. (Right means here to the left of the onlooker and vice versa).

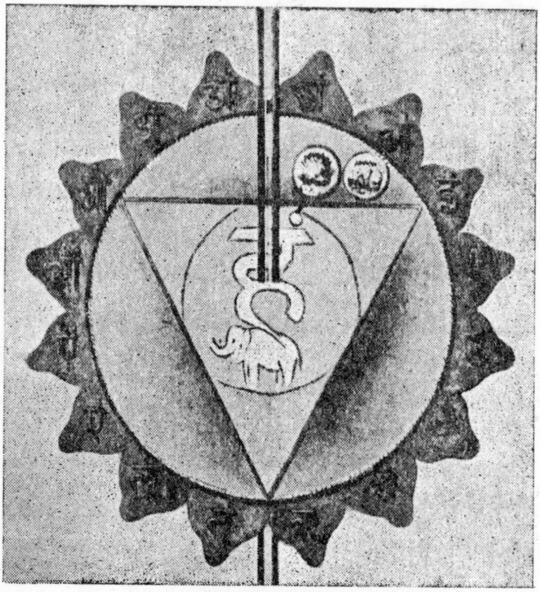

Illustration 9
Viśuddha-Cakra with 16 petals. 16 vowels.

2-petalled lotus

16-petalled lotus
element: ether
animal: elephant

12-petalled lotus
element: air
animal: antelope

10-petalled lotus
element: fire
animal: ram

6-petalled lotus
element: water
animal: makara

4-petalled lotus
element: earth
animal: elephant

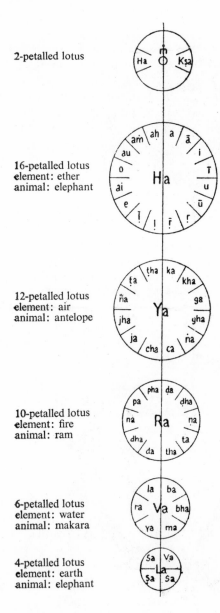

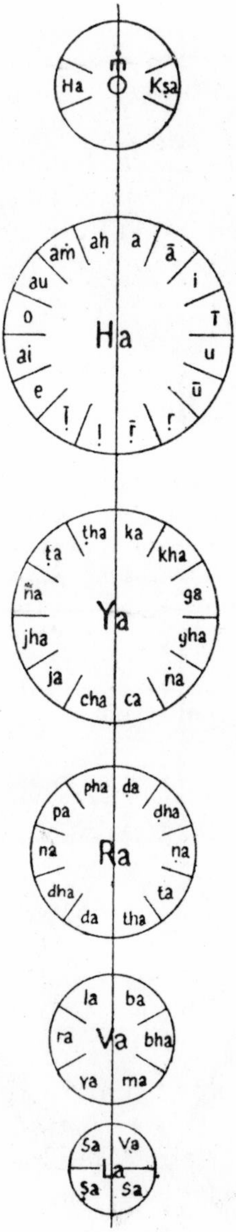

With this distribution of the letters, the sequence of the Devanāgarī letters is given. Only, the beginning of the same lies in the 16-petalled lotus: *a*, *ā*, *i*, *ī*, etc. which continue towards below over all the lotus flowers in which, every time, beginning is made to the right above. Therefore, after *āḥ* (end of the 16-petalled lotus) comes *ka* (beginning of the 12-petalled lotus); after *ṭha* (end of the 12-petalled lotus) follows *ḍa* (beginning of the 10-petalled lotus), etc. upto the last letter (*sa*) in the 4-petalled lotus. The alphabet ends with the letters *Ha* and *Kṣa*. But according to the Tāntric texts, the cultic alphabet in reality consists of 51 letters, of which the last three are *Ha*, *Lla* (cerebral *La*) and *Kṣa*. For a particular purpose, only 50 letters are used, either *Lla* or *Kṣa* being omitted from the original alphabet. The 51-lettered alphabet occurs, unabridged, once in the interior of the 1000-petalled lotus in the form of a *triangle*. The first 16 letters (*a* to *aḥ* form one side of the triangle. The next 16 letters (*ka* to *ta*) form the second, the 16 letters following them (*tha* to *sa*) form the third side of the triangle. The remaining three letters, *Ha*, *Lla*, *Kṣa* are found *inside* the triangle in the three corner points. (cf. *Serpent Power*, p. 485.)

Illustration 10

Survey of the distribution of the letters over the lotus petals.

The position of the Centres

The first centre (Mūlādhāra-Cakra) is found in the region between the genitals and anus; the second centre (Svādhiṣṭhāna-Cakra) is somewhat above the genitals; the third (Maṇipūra-Cakra) is in the region of the navel; the fourth (Anāhata-Cakra) is in the region of the heart; the fifth (Viśuddha-Cakra) is in the region of the larynx; the sixth (Ājñā-Cakra) is situated between the eyebrows; and the seventh centre (Sahasrāra-Cakra) encloses the top part of the head. Every centre is symbolically represented as a lotus with a fixed number of petals (or of "spokes" when the centre is named cakra).[29]

The *sequential series* of the centres and the *number of* their "petals" are as follows:

7 Sahasrāra:	1000 petals
6 Ājñā:	2 petals (Illustration 8)
5 Viśuddha:	16 petals (Illustration 9)
4 Anāhata:	12 petals (Illustration 6)
3 Maṇipūra:	10 petals (Illustration 7)
2 Svādhiṣṭhāna:	6 petals (Illustration 4)
1 Mūlādhāra:	4 petals (Illustration 5)

With the first five lotus flowers are connected the *five classical "Elements"* which are signified by definite geometrical figures (Yantras). They are as follows (see illustrations 4-9):

Lotus	*Element*	*Yantra*
16 petals	"ether" (ākāśa)	Circle
12 petals	"air" (vāyu)	Hexagram*
10 petals	"fire" (tejas)	Triangle (with Svastika-forms)
6 petals	"water" (apaḥ)	Waxing crescent Moon
4 petals	"earth" (pṛthivī)	Square

29 One should take note of the designation "cakras" which, as we shall later see, refer to, besides the centres, also to the "circles in the cosmos".

*Hexagram—figure formed by two intersecting equilateral triangles (the angular points coinciding with those of a hexagon).

Central Sound and peripheral sound

(Illustration 10)

Each element is characterized by a particular sound—made visible with the help of a Devanāgarī letter in the middle of the lotus. We shall name it the "Central Sound" of the lotus (Bījamantra = the seed-sound). The element owes its existence to the central sound. The individual petals of the lotus, too, bear Devanāgarī letters. We shall here speak of the "peripheral sounds".

Bindu or Anusvāra

Above every letter one can see a point (Bindu, Anusvāra). The pronunciation of the letter will, therefore, always ensue as nasalized. This shows that the letters serve a sacred aim in this context.

Devatā and Śakti (Devī)

A Bindu is a place where a *divinity*[30] reveals itself. In the letters themselves there is manifested the shaping *operative force* of this divinity. This is the female (Śakti) while the corresponding god (Devatā) is male. In the Bindu belonging to the central sound *La* (in the four-petalled lotus) a Devatā emerges into manifestation. (See illustration 5). Beside him (marked outside the Bindu), there is a Śakti—the "queen" of this centre. These two central divinities—Devatā and Śakti (who is also called Devī)—form the ruling pair of divinities of this centre. The following four lotus-flowers point each to such a ruling divine pair.

About the nature of this divinity, its kind of appearance in the respective centres, there are detailed descriptions. These, and a lot of other things—for example, the symbolic colours, appearing in the centres; or the qualities of the senses which are connected with the elements; or certain passions and faculties,[31] etc.—must

30 In Hinduism, there is only *one*, uncreated God. The "divinities" which occur in our text are only different ways of appearance and simultaneously they are also special cosmic functions of the one God.

31 With the six-petalled lotus are connected for example the "six foes of man": Kāma (desire, lust), Krodha (anger), Lobha (covetousness), Moha (crror, delusion), Mada (arrogance, pride), Mātsaryya (envy).

be left out of consideration by us in order not to lose sight of the leading thought of our explanation; still, the statements made up to now require the following supplementation:

(1) From a fixed place named "Kanda", in the root of the four petalled lotus, arise the "72000 Nāḍīs", i.e. subtle channels of life-force (Prāṇa). Three of these Nāḍīs possess pivotal importance. They are, namely, Suṣumnā, Iḍā and Piṅgalā. Suṣumnā is the most important among them. It is, in illustration 3a, shown as the line of connection of all the Cakras, while Iḍā and Piṅgalā wind themselves around Suṣumnā like two snakes. Although one cannot say exactly which of the two "serpents" is on the left or the right of Suṣumnā, in the texts, however, Iḍā is always described as current to the left and Piṅgalā as current to the right. Iḍā winds itself from the right testicle up to the left nostril and Piṅgalā from the left testicle up to the right nostril. It is further mentioned that Iḍā is of *lunar* nature, Piṅgalā of *solar* nature and Suṣumnā of *fiery* nature. Iḍā and Piṅgalā form with Suṣumnā and the two petals of the Ājñācakra the *Caduceus of Hermes*.[32] The yogi seeks through resolute practices to gather into Suṣumnā the life forces, otherwise flowing through Iḍā and Piṅgalā. (Out of Suṣumnā, Piṅgalā and Iḍā have once emerged.) With this a state is attained, in which there is "neither day nor night" because "Suṣumnā devours the time".[33]

(2) In the illustrations 3a and 3b, we see between the 2-petalled and the 1000-petalled lotus another 12-petalled lotus which we have not yet mentioned. This lotus does not, however, belong to the main series. The text deals with it in connection with the 1000-petalled lotus. A similar thing holds good for a small 8-petalled lotus-flower below the 12-petalled one (illustration 6).

(3) When we talk of the "six centres", they are meant to be the first six centres without the 1000-petalled lotus which is regarded as the united essence of the lower ones and is raised far above them. The 6 centres are distributed in three groups according to the following scheme:

32 Avalon p. 151.

33 Avalon pp. 229 and 111.

Centre	*Number of petals*	*Group*
6	**2**	III
5	16	
4	**12**	II
3	10	
2	6	I
1	**4**	

Every one of these groups has a sort of a "culminating point" where the cakras, which respectively represent each group, converge. These points are found one after another in the 4-, 12- and 2-petalled lotus. In these places, each time there is found a small triangle as a symbol for the female principle (Trikoṇa, Yoni) in which a liṅgam (phallus) is drawn. In the 4-petalled lotus lies the Kuṇḍalinī-Śakti—the highest manifestation of the creative power in man—which is in deep sleep and which encircles itself around the liṅgam in three and a half circles like a serpent, and it closes with its head the entrance into the Suṣumnā. The triangle representing the female receptive principle and the male creative symbol are red in the 4-petalled lotus, golden in the 12-petalled lotus and white in the 2-petalled lotus. Werner Bohm[34] regards the three unions of the male and female principle as the three steps of love—the physical-elementary, the mental and the spiritual—as corresponding with the Greek ideas—Eros, Philia and Agape.

(4) When we consider the three regions—head, neck and trunk—of man seated in a lotus seat as in illustration 3a and 3b, in the trunk we find the first four cakras with the four classical elements: Earth, Water, Fire and Air. In these cakras are contained all the consonants. The neck is the seat of the 5th lotus centre (with 16 petals) with the Ether-element ("the Quintessence"). Here all *vowels* are to be found. Between the eyebrows there is the 2-petalled flower (lotus). Here, a.o. Manas—the mind—rules; it is not an element in the usual sense, and here we do no more find the divine *pair*. There is to be seen (in illustration 8) one Śakti, with 6 faces, 18 eyes and 6 arms; she is called Hākinī and sits on a white lotus. No (male) Devatā rules

34 Bohm, *op. cit*. p. 60.

here any more; his place is taken over by the yogi himself who has attained freedom (mokṣa). As already mentioned, these 6 lotus-flowers are the 6 actual centres which belong to the human being "personally". The 1000-petalled lotus-flower is already the superhuman in man. In the Tibetan Tantra-system, the 2-petalled lotus and the 1000-petalled lotus are understood as *one* centre.[35] The 2-petalled lotus is, in a certain way, the key to the 1000-petalled lotus. If we count together the petals of the first 6 lotus-flowers —4+6+10+12+16+2—, we arrive at the total of 50. This is the usual number of the letters of the (cultic) Devanāgarī. According to the formulation of Kālīcaraṇa, this alphabet is contained twenty-times in the 1000-petalled lotus.[36] The Sahasrāra-lotus thus is the potentiated sum of the lower lotus-flowers.

Cosmology and aim of the Tantra-Yoga

Now at the conclusion of this introduction, I will briefly deal with the aim of the Kuṇḍalinī-Yoga (which is a particular form of the Tantra-Yoga).

According to the cosmology of the Tantra-Yoga, the man is, in the fullest sense, a microcosm. There is nothing in the universe (macrocosm), which is not in the human body. The creator of the macrocosm as well as of the microcosm is Śabda-Brahman; "Śabda" is a ringing sound. Thus here we speak of Brahman in its function as the "*divine word*". The creative power of Śabda-Brahman (i.e. the substantial power of the word) is *Mahā-Kuṇḍalī* in the macrocosm and the *Kuṇḍalinī* (the coiled

35 cf. Govinda, *Grundlagen tibetischer Mystik* (Basic Principles of Tibetan Mysticism), Zurich 1956, p. 158.

36 As pointed out in the text to illustration 10, the Devanāgarī actually consists of 51 letters. According to Kālīcaraṇa, in connection with the 1000-petalled lotus, *one* letter is omitted, so that the number exactly amounts to 1000. On this he writes (*Serpent Power*, p. 426): "The fiftyone letters cannot be taken to be in the petals of the Sahasrāra. With fiftyone letters repeated twenty times, the number is 1020 and repeated nineteen times is 969. By leaving out Kṣakāra we are freed of this difficulty"; and he sees his assumption confirmed by the following text: "The Great Lotus Sahasrāra is white and has its head downward and the lustrous letters from Akāra (A) ending with the last letter before Kṣakāra (Kṣa) decorate it". We shall return to this problem later on. (See page 55ff.).

up) in the microcosm. This aspect of the Śabda-Brahman is the divine Mother of the universe: Mahā-Śakti or Mahā-Devī. Behind the creation stands a consciousness —the most comprehensive consciousness which exists, called Cit or Saṁvit. This aspect of Śabda-Brahman is also named under the name of Śiva. Śiva is described as the unchangeable static aspect of the great consciousness, while Śakti represents the dynamic, active side of the same consciousness. It is Śakti who has created the five elements (Mahābhūtas) from the finest (Ākāśa) to the grossest (Pṛthivī). The gradual condensation of the primordial substance (Prakṛti) implies, from the point of the creating Śakti, a stepwise cramping, a growing renunciation with regard to fully unfolded "Being".[37] When the earth-element is created, Śakti has sacrificed herself to the maximum limit; she cannot do more; with this her creative power has reached the end. In her last emanation, the earth-element, she lies rolled together and sleeps. This aspect of Śakti is the Kuṇḍalinī. But there is a whole series of other aspects of Śakti, still active, which in some way keep alive the former stages of the route to the 4-petalled lotus. Thus in the human body as well as in the cosmos, there are active innumerable Śaktis which are nothing but the forms of manifestation of the one primordial Śakti. The six centres are to be considered as the main stages of Śakti on her way from heaven (microcosmically: the region of the head, the 2-and 1000-petalled lotus) to earth (microcosmically: the 4-petalled lotus).

The 1000-petalled lotus is the region of pure, undimmed consciousness and is thus the realm of Śiva, which is also the proper home of Śakti. The many richly differentiated worlds which are situated in the macrocosm as well as in the microcosm, owe their existence solely to the fact that Śiva and Śakti, regarded from a certain standpoint, are no more one but are separated from each other, as a result of the "emigration" of Śakti out of her spiritual home into the earthly region of gross matter. This emigration brought with it also the gradual, step-by-step veiling of the primordial consciousness; therefore, the Kuṇḍalinī-Śakti is also named Māyā-Śakti (Māyā = illusion). The yogi endeavours to

37 The German word "Sein" is here translated in correspondence with the translation of the "Sein" of Parmenides in the second dissertation of this book. It is used as the term for the "essence of existence".

overcome this illusion in its almost unlimited effects. He wants to incorporate his personal consciousness again into the universal divine consciousness, to "repatriate" himself, because the yogi knows that he once participated in the great divine consciousness, but that he has lost this participation.

The yogi now attains to his goal by waking up, with the help of the method of the Kuṇḍalinī-Yoga, the serpent sleeping in the 4-petalled lotus and makes it ascend upwards. Thus the creation is step-by-step made retrograde. On its way towards above, the awakened serpent re-absorbs everything that had been created through its earlier descent. The earth-element is, first, carried back to its seed-sound *laṁ*, called by us the "central sound", out of which it once originated.[38] This seed-sound will then be dissolved into the element "water" which is again changed in its seed-sound *vaṁ* which now forms the body of the Kuṇḍalinī-serpent. When the serpent climbs up further, the sound *vaṁ* is dissolved into the "fire-element" and this again is changed into the sound *raṁ*, which at this moment forms the body of the Kuṇḍalinī-serpent. Thus, it goes on further, not only the elements and seed-sounds, but everything that is in the respective lotuses being dissolved. To this belong all the finer differentiations of the sounds, as the peripheral sounds, beside this the ruling gods and their operations and so also the sense-qualities: smelling, tasting, seeing, touching, hearing and even the thinking. All this is reabsorbed by the ascending Kuṇḍalinī-Śakti who releases herself step by step, until finally she unites with Śiva in the 1000-petalled lotus—an event which the yogi experiences as the highest ecstasy (Samādhi). The body of the yogi then becomes corpselike, cold and stiff. Only the region on the top of his head, where Śiva and Śakti celebrate their wedding, remains warm.[39] In general, the yogi cannot remain in Samādhi for a long time: a natural impulse leads the Kuṇḍalinī-Śakti, again, step by step below so that little by little the reabsorbed worlds are

38 cf. above, p. 32 (on central sound and peripheral sound).

39 On account of this process of stepwise dissolution of all creation, in the microcosm, this form of Yoga is called Laya-Yoga (Laya=dissolution). According to the Tantra cosmology the same process will once be carried out in the macrocosm: Mahā-Kuṇḍalī will awaken and in its ascent, all its creations will be withdrawn (causing the dissolution of the world—Mahā-Pralaya).

newly created. The body of the yogi becomes again "alive" and warm, the senses return back, and the yogi again finds himself in the multiple distorted world of illusion (of which *one* token is "multiplicity" of all that is existing).

What is to remark is this: While the great Śakti cramps herself step by step on her way from the heaven to the earth, the macrocosmic and the microcosmic "worlds" arise. When on the other hand, that Śakti, through the methods of Yoga, wakes up from her Kuṇḍalinī-state and ascends upwards, releasing herself little by little, the worlds are bound to disappear in the same degree. The "Being" *here* implies at the same time a "Non-Being" *there* and *vice versa*. The "dissolution" of the microcosmic world experienced by the yogi is a "dissolution" as seen from one side only; juxtaposed against it, there is a "coming into Being" in the spiritual world.

The cosmology of the Tantra-Yoga is so difficult to understand for Westerners and so incompatible in its essentials with their way of thinking that it would require a bulky volume to present it to them in a manner which, to a certain degree, precludes all misunderstandings. In this short description it has been attempted to signify, at least to some small extent, the "milieu", in which the lotus-flowers have first found their home of origin.

But one may ask, what have these lotus-flowers to do with astronomy and even with Gestalt-Astronomy ? The ground for answer to this question will be prepared in the next section by pointing to the occurrence and significance of the symbolism of the seven centres existing in other traditions.

(*ii*) Parallelisms to the Symbolism of the Seven Lotus-Flowers in other Traditions

The symbolism of the seven centres of the Kuṇḍalinī-Yoga is not found to be an isolated phenomenon. It has parallels in other Hindu traditions, in the Mithra-Mysteries, the Gnosis and Western mysticism.

Saundaryalaharī

In this famous Indian Sanskrit poem[40] which is ascribed to the

40 This work has appeared in a distinguished edition (Sanskrit/English): *The Saundaryalaharī* or *Flood of Beauty*, edited, translated and presented

great Śaṅkarācārya (7th Century A.D.), there is also found the lore of the seven cakras. We cannot deal with this work in all the details but shall confine ourselves to the following conclusions:

(1) All the known centres of the Kuṇḍalinī-Yoga occur in the poem (i.e. Mūlādhāra, Svādhiṣṭhāna, etc.)

(2) But while these centres have been designated in the Yoga-system as cakras *and* as padmas, in the *Saundaryalaharī* there is mention *only* of the cakras ("circles"), with one exception: The Sahasrāra is called, as in Yoga, a "thousand-petalled *lotus*". This lotus assumes an exceptional place among the remaining cakras, all of which once arose out of it. We have seen how in the yoga as well, the 1000-petalled is no ordinary lotus but represents the "super-human in man".[41] The special place of the 1000-petalled lotus becomes explicit in the *Saundaryalaharī* also through the fact that the Ājñā-Cakra has been named as the first cakra (and not the 1000-petalled lotus), the Viśuddha-Cakra as the second and finally the Mūlādhāra-Cakra as the sixth. (Here also is seen a difference from the Yoga-system in which the enumeration begins at the other end: Mūlādhāra is the first cakra and Ājñā the sixth.)

(3) Suprisingly, the cakras in the *Saundaryalaharī* are in no way concerned with eventual centres in men, but *exclusively with the circles or spheres in the universe.* The universe is understood as the body of the divine world-mother Mahā-Devī; it has developed once out of a pre-world primordial condition (sahasrāra) and after six cosmic steps, of which the first corresponds to the Ājñā-Cakra, it has come to be what we call the universe today. For us, this last transmission is important in so far as the names of

in photographs by W. Norman Brown, Cambridge, Mass., 1958. Brown says the following in his foreword about the significance of this poem: "This work is one of the most widely used devotional texts of modern Hinduism. Many people employ it daily throughout the year; large numbers know some or all of its stanzas by heart. Manuscripts of it abound in every part of the country—north, south, east, west, central—and it is one of the relatively few works which have been embellished with manuscript-paintings. There are numerous lists of magic diagrams (yantra) and mystic seed syllables (bījākṣara) for use with the separate stanzas and prescriptions of accessory paraphernalia and methods of reciting the stanzas···"

41 It may be mentioned that the work referred to above is called *Ṣaṭ-cakra-nirūpaṇa*, i.e. "The description of the *six* cakras", although *seven* centres are described.

the previously described seven centres in men are referred to here distinctly and only as the *cosmical spheres in the universe.* But when one remembers the extraordinary interest which was brought to bear on the movements of the heavens in ancient times in all cultures,[42] then one may ask whether the seven cosmic regions of the *Saundaryalaharī* are not, perhaps, apart from their mystical contents, related also to the external visible phenomena of the sky viz. the movements of the seven planets.

This question cannot be answered with certainty on the basis of *Saundaryalaharī* alone. Here nothing more than a general superficial analogy between the seven cakras on the one hand and seven planets on the other, can be posited.

We must, therefore, get the more interested in another sevenfold system—the Yoga-system, which carries the same names as the system of the *Saundaryalaharī*, but which is incomparably much more differentiated in its composition than the latter. As a matter of fact, as will be shown in the next section, it is this, more detailed, differentiation inside the cakra-system which renders it possible for us to answer with certainty the question raised above. But first, we shall turn to some other traditions in order to round off to some extent our considerations in this behalf.

*The Cult of Mithra and the Gnosis**

Franz Cumont writes in his book *The Mysteries of Mithra*[43]

42 Franz Boll (lectures in the winter-semester 1922/23) in *Kleine Schriften zur Sternkunde des Altertums* ("Brief writings on the knowledge of the Stars of ancient times), Leipzig 1950, p. 371) says the following on this topic: "The history of the belief in stars in a higher sense is a unitary, homogeneous structure. In no other religion such a unitariness of ideas over the widest spheres of the earth is established. Above all, it became the common possession of all religions of the mediterranean region and of Near East and reached also, in its radiating influence, far towards Eastern Asia. Christianity, the East and the West—all are connected in this belief in a great continuity of spiritual life, in spite of Spengler's contrary assertions. No fact of spiritual life can demonstrate such continuity better than the history of belief in the Stars...". And in another place of this lecture (p. 371) it is said: "In the worship of the stars, there is a direct connection between religion and science. Already the Babylonian priests appear to have represented both; since their days, side by side, with the belief in the Stars, there goes on the attempt at scientific mastery of the knowledge of the celestial bodies.."

*Gnosis means knowledge of spiritual mysteries, in general. In particular it is the name for a philosophical-mystic tradition of the Near East.

43 *Die Mysterien des Mithra*, German edition ed. by Georg Gehrich, Leipzig/Berlin 1923.

as follows: "The seven steps of Initiation which the mystic has to undergo in order to attain perfect wisdom and purity, correspond in this cult to the spheres of the seven planets."[44] "The heavens are divided into 7 spheres, each of which is allotted to one planet. A sort of a ladder which consists of 8 gates situated one above the other, of which the seven first are composed of seven metals,[45] serves in the temple as a symbolic reminder of the way which had to be traversed or travelled in order to attain to the topmost region of the fixed stars. In fact, one had to pass each time through a gate in order to reach from one floor to the next, a gate guarded by an angel of Oromazd. Only the mystics, who had been taught the particular formulae with this special aim, knew how to placate these exacting guards. The further the soul advanced through those different zones, the more it shed off, like clothes, the passions and faculties which it had received on its way down to the earth. It left to the Moon its forces of life and nutrition, to Mercury its avaricious propensities, to Venus its erotic hankerings, to the Sun its intellectual faculties, to Mars its courage of a warrior, to Jupiter its ambitious desires, to Saturn its propensity towards inertia. It was naked, freed from all deficiencies and all sensuality, when it attained to the real heaven where the gods dwelt, in order to enjoy endless bliss as an elevated being in eternal light."[46]

In the book by Franz Boll,[47] one comes across the following passage: "The fatalistic view of later antiquity expresses distinctly the same thing. It allows man to be ruled by those gods of the stars or planets not only in his physical but also in his spiritual and moral existence. When the soul which is of divine origin and is, therefore, supposed to go back to heaven again, descends down into the captivity of the earthly body, then it receives the fatal gifts from the seven planets—the seven mortal sins of the middle ages which, in the gnostic teaching, are considered as foreign devils dwelling in the soul. Each planet grants one of them..." on account of which "that pessimistic impulse arises, according

44 *op. cit.* p. 129.

45 The publication of a special essay dealing with the seven metals from the standpoint of an archaic natural science is planned.

46 Cumont, *op. cit.* p. 130.

47 Boll, *op. cit.* p. 199 f. Cf. on the same theme also Will-Erich Peuckert, *Astrologie*, Stuttgart 1960, p. 129.

to which the journey of the soul through the planets, is a fall of man and the gifts of the planets are nothing but vices."

Rightly has Julius Schwabe in his *Archetype and Zodiac*[48] instituted a comparison between the systems of Kuṇḍalinī-Yoga on the one hand and of the Mithra-Mysteries on the other: "What is aspired after, in the Mithra-Mysteries, with the symbolic ascent through the seven cosmic storeys is attained by the Kuṇḍalinī-yogi because he lets the serpent (Kuṇḍalinī) ascend up in his own trunk and head, which are equated with the cosmos, until his marriage union with Śiva. And as the aspirant in the Mithra-Mysteries at every step lays aside and returns back his passions and faculties, which he had once come to possess during his descent to the earth..., so also the centres of force and consciousness are reduced by the yogi one after the other and dissolved in the next higher centre."

It can hardly be doubted that in both the systems, the same topic is basically dealṭ with. Only the question is: how far does this identity hold good ? Does it hold good to such a degree that, in concrete terms, the four-petalled lotus in the Yoga-system is identical with the Moon in the Mithra-system, the six-petalled lotus with Mercury, the ten-petalled lotus with Venus, the twelve-petalled lotus with the Sun, the sixteen-petalled lotus with Mars, the two-petalled lotus with Jupiter and the thousand-petalled lotus with Saturn? Is there not only a general analogy between the two systems but also a detailed correspondence ?

Western Mysticism

We come across the first reference to the fact that such a correspondence really consists, in illustration 11, reproduced here from the *Theosophia Practica*[49] of the famous mystic Johann Georg Gichtel (1638-1710), a pupil of Jakob Boehme.

This figure shows that the European mystic also knows the doctrine of seven centres localised in the human body, which

48 *Archetyp und Tierkreis*, Basel 1951, p. 292 ff.

49 1st edition 1696; after a note in the later edition of 1736, the pictures in the book (whose text comprises mainly a commentary on the figures) was printed only about 10 years after the death of Gichtel, i.e. about the year 1720. The corresponding figure in the French translation of *Theosophia Practica* (Bibliothèque Charconac, Paris 1897) serves as the pattern for illustration 11.

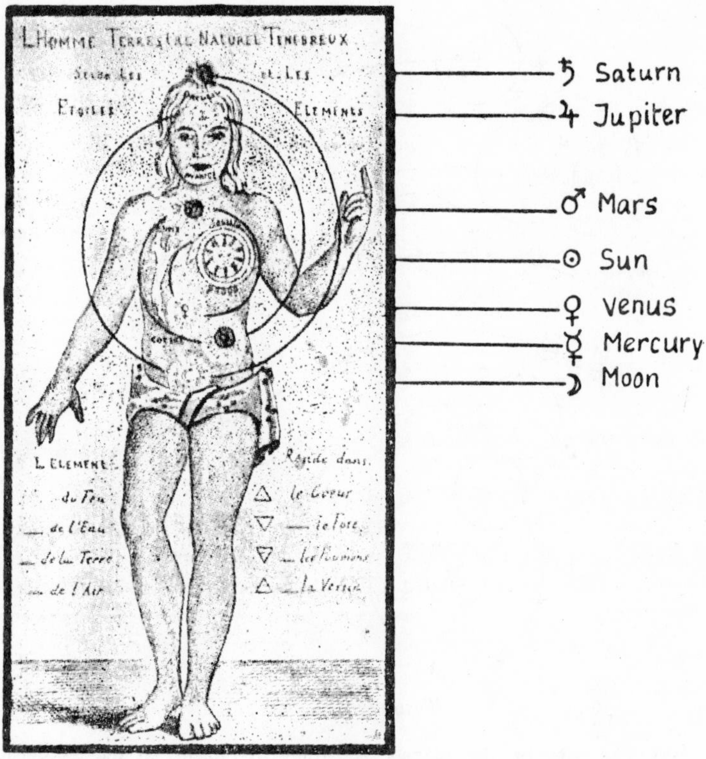

Illustration 11

Figure from the book "Theosophia Practica" by J. G. Gichtel. The order of the planets is that of Ptolemy: Saturn, Jupiter, Mars, Sun, Venus Mercury, Moon.

agree to a great extent, with the Indian ones. But, while in the Yoga-system, the seven centres are represented as "lotus-flowers", each with a definite number of petals, Gichtel, on the other hand, employs the seven planets. His order of the planets, which begins in the human body with the Moon and ends with Saturn in the uppermost part of the head, corresponds exactly with the sequence of the "storeys or floors" in the Mithra-cult, through which the soul has to travel during its ascent. This sequence of the series, as one finds in illlustration 12, is the order of the series of the planets according to Ptolemy.

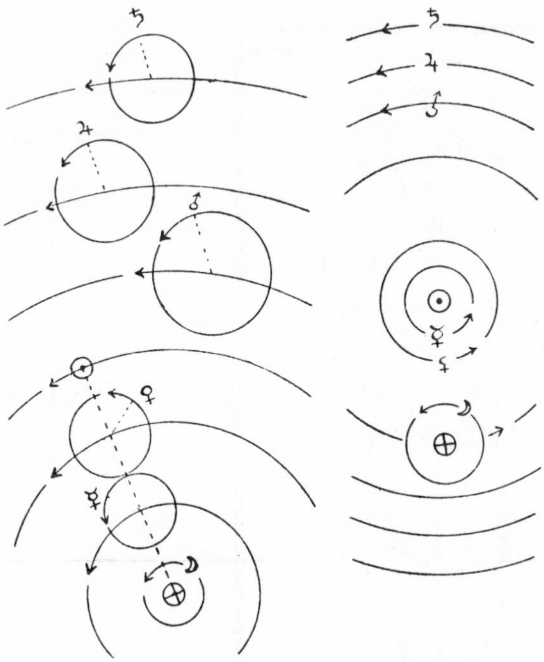

a b

Illustration 12

(a) The order of the planets according to Ptolemy in the geocentric world-system.

(b) The order of the planets in the heliocentric world system.

Both the diagrammatic representations are not to scale.

It is worth noticing that the "three worlds in man" are spoken of in the book of Gichtel as also in the Indian texts. In the *Ṣaṭ-cakra-nirūpaṇa* for example, the Nirvāṇa-Śakti (one of the many aspects of the Mahā-Śakti), is called "the mother of the three worlds" while Puruṣa (one aspect of the divine creator) is described as "the one who was before the three worlds". (Verse 38). In the body, the 6 lotus-flowers are the centres of the three worlds, while the 1000-petalled lotus expresses what was *before* the three worlds. Let us compare this to what we find in the observation of Gichtel on the title-page of his book: "A short explanation of the three principles of the three worlds in man, represented in clear illustrations which show how and where they have their respective centres in the inner man; according to what the author in his divine contemplation has found in himself and what he has felt, experienced and perceived."

The order of the planets according to Ptolemy

Consider the *heliocentric* system. If one were to leave the earth and travel to Saturn, the journey would, as the planets are shown, first take us to the Moon, then to Venus, thereafter to Mercury, and then, in this sequence, to the Sun, Mars, Jupiter and, finally, to Saturn.

If we now consider the system of *Ptolemy*, it strikes us that here after the Moon, there follows immediately Mercury, and only then Venus. Then, everything follows as before: there follow one after another the Sun, Mars, Jupiter and Saturn. Why are Mercury and Venus interchanged in the system of Ptolemy ? This question requires a treatise which here would lead too far. But we can briefly suggest an essential part of the answer. Mercury and Venus are interchanged because the system of Ptolemy does not represent a *spatial* system but a *temporal* system. Spatially, Mercury is, no doubt, more distant from the earth than Venus, but the *period of revolution* of Mercury lies between the periods of revolution of the Moon and Venus, as can be seen from the following arrangement:

Siderical revolution (revolution related to the system of the fixed stars)			*Synodical revolution* (revolution related to the Sun)		
Moon	$27\frac{1}{3}$	days	Moon	$29\frac{1}{2}$	days
Mercury	88	days	Mercury	116	days
Venus	225	days	Venus	584	days

This middle position of Mercury results also from illustration 12a: the circle of revolution (epicycle) of Mercury lies, with respect to its size, between the corresponding orbits of Moon and Venus.

We can now pass on to the third section, in which we shall demonstrate that the planet system of Ptolemy localized by

Gichtel in man is, as a matter of fact, *identical* with the seven-fold cakra-system of the Kuṇḍalinī-Yoga localized in man, as considered from a purely astronomical standpoint. We need not be excited by the fact that in both the cases, astronomical facts appear to have been localized *in the human body*: This manner of representation corresponds with the deep-rooted and widespread view of man held in ancient times,—man as microcosmos and cosmos as macroanthropos (macrocosmic man), whereby both the cosmoi correspond formally as a whole as well as in all their parts to each other. Important for us above all, is to ascertain that in the cakra-system, the astronomical knowledge of those ancient times has been fixed up. We can consider the localization in the body as such, as an archaic convention[50] with which we need not deal further here. It remains only to deal with the astronomy implicitly contained in the ancient teachings and to elaborate it in its essential features.

(*iii*) The Seven Lotus-Flowers and the Number of their Petals as an Archaic Representation of the Gestalt-Astronomy according to the System of Ptolemy

In the following discussion, we distinguish between two kinds of astronomical numbers: 1) the *period-numbers* and 2) the *gestalt-numbers*. The first differentiate themselves from the latter through the fact that they are dependent on certain selected units (temporal units: day, week, month, year, etc.), while the gestalt-numbers are independent of any kind of units. Thus, for example, the time of the revolution of the Moon is a fixed period. This period amounts to 28 days or 4 weeks or one month, etc. The appertaining period-numbers are 28, 4, 1, that is to say, there are as many period-numbers as there are units of time. In the period of four weeks, the Moon appears in different phases. If we bring together in our thought the four places in the sky which correspond to the main phases, i.e. the three visible main phases and the new-moon phase which is invisible, we get a definite figure: a regular square.

50 I hope to explain in detail in another work that it is, as a matter of fact, more than a mere convention. The attentive reader will himself find in some places the necessary clues hereto.

The four-number, gained in this way, we call a *gestalt-number*. Exactly speaking, here we deal with a "spatially fixed temporal form". It is, like a melody, a successive, i.e. a temporal form, because it appears only in the course of time. Through the spatial fixation, it gains qualities of a simultaneous or spatial form. *The time-units have no influence on the gestalt-number* 4: *the figure "square" remains enduring, notwithstanding the time-unit which has been employed.*

In his doctrine of the stages of human age-periods (Tetrabiblos) also *Ptolemy* connects the Moon with the number 4. But here they are four years.[51] Franz Boll makes the following remark on it: "And when Ptolemy finds the Tetraeteris (square) suitable for the Moon, he could have well thought of the 4 phases of the Moon, and also may have remembered that the old "Great Year" of 8 years, i.e. the old compensation period between the courses of the Sun and the Moon, was temporally divided into two halves...."[52] Here we see two entirely different derivations of the number four: the "Great Year" of 8 years is, as we shall show, a period-number, while the number of 4 is a gestalt-number on the basis of the four phases of the Moon.

We shall now consider the 7 planets in the sequential order of Ptolemy from these two points of view. It will, thereby, be shown that all the numbers mentioned by Ptolemy are the *period-numbers*, astronomically demonstrable, for the first six planets (Moon to Jupiter), as a characterization of the stages of the human life-span, whereas, at the same time, the 6 centres in man with the respective number of lotus-petals described by the Yoga represent nothing else than *the same sequential order of Ptolemy*,

51 The stages of age-periods are coordinated to the planets, according to the sequence of Ptolemy:

The period of the *Moon* embraces the period of **4** *years* of life (1-4)

The period of *Mercury* embraces the period of **10** *years* of life (5-14)

The period of *Venus* embraces the period of **8** *years* of life (15-22)

The period of the *Sun* embraces the period of **19** *years* of life (23-41)

The period of *Mars* embraces the period of **15** *years* of life (42-56)

The period of *Jupiter* embraces the period of **12** *years* of life (57-68)

The period of *Saturn* stretches from **68** *life-years* up to the end of life. Ptolemy here mentions *no number*.

52 Franz Boll, *op. cit.* p. 196.

but this time from the stand-point of also astronomically demonstrable gestalt-numbers of the planets concerned.

In the second part of his essay on "The Ages of Life"[53] in which Franz Boll deals with the corresponding section of Ptolemy's "Tetrabiblos", he makes a remark that the "cycle of Mercury (ten years)", mentioned by Ptolemy, were "provisionally without an astronomically demonstrable basis", although Ptolemy himself had pointed out this cycle "...as the half of a 20-year-cycle of Mercury".

The required astronomical proof has not yet been given and I have always learnt from the astronomers of our time that they cannot imagine any 20-year-cycle of Mercury. We shall see soon that there actually is such a 20-year-cycle of Mercury, but that it can only be proved in the frame of Gestalt-Astronomy as a striking and independent phenomenon.

Let us first consider the Moon from the view of Gestalt-Astronomy.

Moon

We found that the Moon is connected with the form of a square. This is the *primary* pattern which forms itself and strikes the attention of the observer of the sky. But the Moon forms also another pattern which was well-known to the ancients. We have better cite here what Kepler has said about it in 1603 in his *Judgement on the Fiery Triangle*[54] (The relations between Jupiter and Saturn, mentioned in the following quotation, will be explained later on, see page 54ff.)

"6. Can there be no proper reason which would always unite trianglewise three signs ? Answer: We have a good ground to make 12 divisions, namely because in every year, a full and new moon appears in every sign: so we have also good reason to pay attention to the triangle. Because Saturn and Jupiter—the two highest planets—meet one another always over the third part of the Zodiac: therefore, in the lifetime of

53 In *op. cit.* p. 196 "Ein Beitrag zur antiken Ethologie und zur Geschichte der Zahlen" (A contribution to the antique Ethology and to the history of numbers).

54 *Judicium de Trigono igneo*, ed. Frisch I, 444.

every man, three signs are always subjected to such a triangle and they have the most powerful influence in the nativity or horoscope. To this belongs also the position of the Moon in the beginning of the year. Because when he is in Aries this year, he is in the other year in Leo, the third in Sagittarius or Capricorn.

"7. How it does happen that those positions, under which Jupiter and Saturn come together, stand situated with one another trianglewise ?

"8. Which, then, may be properly the beginning of the fiery triangle ?

"9. What advantages may the fiery triangle have over other triangles as important qualities ?

"Answer: Firstly, the most important cardinal point (the spring-equinox). Accordingly it concerns the most memorable times: so much guidance is given to us by historians. Because every triangle has about 200 years, each comes again after 800 years."

Before we get closer into Kepler's text, some remarks may be interjected on the composition of the system of the Zodiac, for those who are not sufficiently at home. The reader, who is not acquainted with astrology or astronomy, may have some difficulties with the quotation of Kepler and with the following remarks on the composition of the Zodiac. He should, however, not be discouraged, but continue his reading. The principle of the astronomical composition of successive forms will still become clear to him.

Little Excursus on the Composition of the Zodiac

Aries and Libra form an axis as also Taurus and Scorpio. The tradition speaks of a special classification of every planet under a particular sign of the Zodiac, expressed through the idea of the "governance" (or "rulership") and another kind of classification, expressed through the designation "exaltation". From the Gestalt-Astronomy, there falls here an interesting light on the Taurus-Scorpio-axis, or replaced by the corresponding planets, on the Venus/Moon—Mars axis, resp.

One should consider first in this context that the signs of the Zodiac, have nothing to do directly with the constellations and their similar names ("Aries" or "Ram", "Taurus" or "Bull", etc.), but represent their own complete system in which nothing else than our solar system becomes manifest in 12 constituents of its inner dynamics, relating to the Earth.*

Only secondarily were named the groups of fixed stars *according to the signs of the Zodiac* but the signs of the Zodiac never got their names from the constellations !

In conclusion, I summarize synoptically the astrological system as it is found in the Tetrabiblos of Ptolemy:

Signs of the Zodiac	*Governance*	*Exaltation*	*Element*	*Sex*
Aries (Meṣa)	Mars	Sun	Fire	male
Taurus (Vṛṣabha)	Venus	Moon	Earth	female
Gemini (Mithuna)	Mercury		Air	male
Cancer (Karka)	Moon	Jupiter	Water	female
Leo (Siṁha)	Sun		Fire	male
Virgo (Kanyā)	Mercury	Mercury	Earth	female
Libra (Tula)	Venus	Saturn	Air	male
Scorpio (Vṛścika)	Mars		Water	female
Sagittarius (Dhanu)	Jupiter		Fire	male
Capricorn (Makara)	Saturn	Mars	Earth	female
Aquarius (Kuṁbha)	Saturn		Air	male
Pisces (Mīna)	Jupiter	Venus	Water	female

*One should remember that in Europe only sāyana-Zodiac is the common Zodiac System.

Now we can elucidate the utterance of Kepler: We seek in a table of the planets the place of the Moon in the beginning of every year. First, for example, the year 1937; after that the year 1938, etc.:

1st January 1937 around midday: Moon 5° Virgo
1st January 1938 around midday: Moon 7° Capricorn
1st January 1939 around midday: Moon 11° Taurus.

If we connect these points (see illustration 13), a *triangle* arises which, therewith, forms itself in three years. The signs of the Zodiac connected here—Virgo-Capricorn-Taurus—form the so-called Earth-Trigon (triangle).

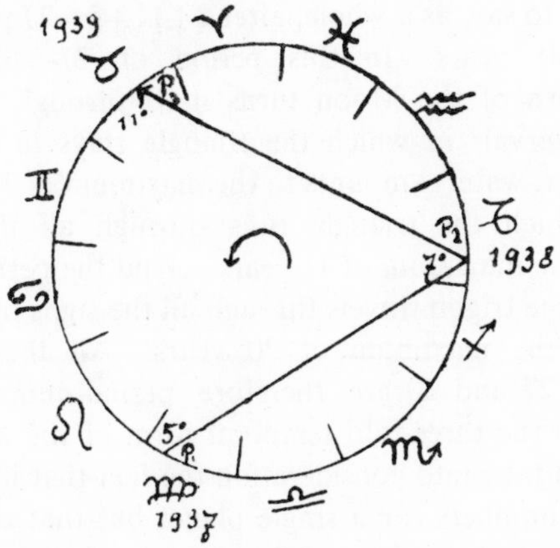

Illustration 13

This second form of the Moon is, therefore, a triangle, the gestalt-number is "3", the period-number belonging to it, when one chooses the year as time-unit, is likewise "3".

Now this triangle does not stand still, it rotates in the Zodiac. First, the element "earth" was the place of abode of the moon-triangle, then the "water"-element becomes the next abode and the "fire"-element the next respectively. This triangle therewith forms itself in the west-east direction, while the rotation of the whole Trigon ensues also in west-east direction.

The time in which *one* corner (P_1) moves itself until it comes to a place where there was the next corner (P_2) previously, amounts to either 8 *years* (which is, therefore, the previously mentioned ancient "Great Year") or—today obviously less known 11 *years*. The trigon has then turned itself approximately by the third part of the circle of the Zodiac. One has, therefore, to take into consideration the following: While *one* point of the trigon moves itself further in 8 years, the one next to it requires 11 years. The same point which first came forward in 8 years, requires, perhaps, next time, 11 years. The triangle is thus an *elastic* triangle, whose points move with varying speed. After further 11 or 8 years, the first-named point is again pushed forward by about a third of the periphery of the circle, that is to say, after 8+11=19 (or 11+8=19) years, reckoned from the beginning. This cycle is known under name of *Meton's Cycle*. Again 8 or 11 years later, the point stands again in its starting-point, that is to say, as a whole, after 8+11+8=27 years or after 11+8+11=30 years. In this period of 27—30 years, the triangle-pattern of the Moon turns itself through the Zodiac. The time-interval in which the triangle stays in one element (fire, earth, air, water) amounts to the maximum of 3 years. The period in which the triangle runs through all the elements amounts to the maximum of 11 years. And the period, in which *one* point of the trigon travels through all the signs of the Zodiac, amounts to the maximum of 30 years. All these numbers: 3, 8, 11, 19, 27 and 30 are, therefore, period-numbers,[55] which are related to the three-fold temporal form of the Moon.

One should take into consideration the fact that in astronomy, there are no numbers for a single planet but that the traditionally obtained numbers always relate to a particular planet *in its relation to another*, in most cases, in its relation to the Sun. The four-fold temporal form of the Moon, formed in a month, for example concerns the Moon in its relation to the Sun. But in this case, it deals primarily with the Moon, not with the Sun. If we would reverse the facts and inquire into the temporal pattern of the Sun in relation to the Moon, we must investigate, instead of the revolution of the Moon, the revolution of the *Sun*. The result would be a 12-fold pattern in the frame of the Zodiac (see later under "Sun"). Concerning the Zodiac, I would again

55 Compare with this the results of the corresponding "Chain-fraction-development" as it is carried out for example, by F. X. Kugler in his book *Sternkunde und Sterndienst in Babel*, Vol. 2, part 2, number 2, p. 422 ff. Kugler points out, besides, the actual usage of the 8 year cycle (from 528-505), of the 27-year-cycle (504-383) and 19-year-cycle (from 382 starting) in Babel.

submit the following clarification: here are never meant the 12 constellations; on the contrary, we always talk of the ecliptic circle divided into 12 equal sections and beginning from the spring-equinox. The axis, which connects the spring-equinox with the autumnal-equinox is the dividing line between the equatorial plane and the ecliptic plane. If the two planes would coincide, there would be no beginning of our Zodiac; the four Cardinal Points would not exist; in short, there would be no Zodiac at all. This Zodiac, separated from the sky of fixed stars, exhibits exclusively a Sun-Earth relation and nothing else. Localisation in the Zodiac involves a reference to this Sun-Earth relation. We stand here entirely on the foundation of astronomy of Ptolemy.[56]

The Sun (in relation to the Moon and Jupiter)

Every month a conjunction or opposition respectively between the Sun and the Moon takes place, and this each time at a 12th part of the circle further ahead. Therefore the gestalt-number of the Sun with reference to the Moon is "12".

Let us again bring to our mind: The gestalt-number of the Moon with reference to the Sun is 4, that of the Sun with reference to the Moon is 12. To this, also belongs the gestalt-number of *Jupiter* with reference to the Sun: this is, namely, likewise 12. As in one cycle of the Sun, 12 Sun-Moon-meetings take place, so also exactly take place 12 Jupiter-Sun-meetings in one Jupiter-cycle. I would like to point, in this context, to the astrological tradition which puts the Moon as governor of Cancer and Jupiter as exalted in Cancer.[57] Not less old is the tradition, in the frame of the doctrine of the correspondence of the macro-microcosmos, which identifies the 12 pairs of ribs with Cancer and the heart enveloped by the ribs with the sign Leo. The signs of the Zodiac Cancer and Leo, *temporally successive*, are here comprehended *spatially* so that the Leo forms the centre of Cancer. As is well known, the Sun is governor of Leo and thus we have brought together in the signs Cancer and Leo, with the planets Moon, Jupiter and Sun belonging to them, all the components of gestalt-number 12 (see illustration 14).

56 cf. *Tetrabiblos* I, 22, in Loeb Classical Library, London, Cambridge (Mass) pp. 109-111.

57 cf. Ptolemy, *Tetrabiblos*, I, pp. 79-91; cf. also the synopsis p. 76.

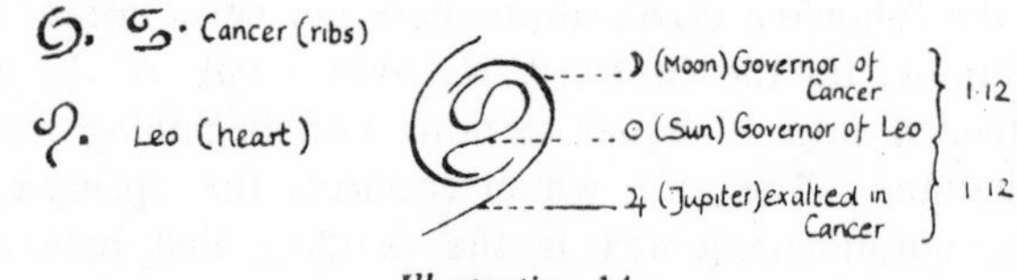

Illustration 14

In this place the yogi localizes the 4th centre, Anâhata-Cakra with the 12 petals. Gichtel puts in this place the Sun. Ptolemy in his periods of human age connects the number 19 with the Sun, which, as Franz Boll rightly recognized, represents nothing else than *Meton's Cycle* which is a *period-number* concerned with the Sun-Moon-relation.

Jupiter and Saturn

We shall now consider the conjunction of Jupiter and Saturn of which Kepler speaks. In every 20th year, such a conjunction takes place, each time by a third of the periphery of the circle further ahead (i.e. in the East-West direction). Thus in 3×20 years $= 60$ years, another trigon forms itself.[58]

As already mentioned by Kepler, the "Great Trigon" remains 200 years long in an element, e.g. in the fire-element (Moon-Trigon, at the most 3 years). In order to travel through the 4 elements, the trigon requires $4 \times 200 = 800$ years (Moon-Trigon: at the most 11 years). In order to come through the total signs of the Zodiac, a point requires 3 x $800 = 2400$ years. In this period, the trigon rotates once in the Zodiac (Moon-Trigon: at the most 30 years). In contrast to the elastic Moon-Triangle, the Jupiter-Saturn-Triangle is reliable and exact in a high degree. What holds good for one point, holds good also for the other points.

58 Thibaut writes about this 60 years cycle thus: "The 60 years Jupiter-cycle described by Varāhamihira and in the works of the third period belongs, according to its origin, to this period. Every year of this cycle carries its own name. The entire cycle is divided in 12 Lustres whose individual components bear the name of the year of the well-known 5 years Yuga (Samvatsara, Parivatsara, etc.). It might be assumed that this 60-year-cycle originated out of the fact that one wished to have together at the same time the 12 years Jupiter-cycle and the 5 years Yuga comprised in a greater period." One discovers that Thibaut has not paid attention to the astronomical proof of this 60 years cycle and therewith to the role which Saturn plays in the coming into existence of the cycle.

From our point of view, the following is important: The whole trigon travels through the 4 elements in 800 years. Between two conjunctions there are 20 years. Let us, for systematical reasons, write this as follows:

Between 2 conjunctions there are $1 \times 20 = 20$ years. We can continue:

between 3 conjunctions there are $2 \times 20 = 40$ years,
between 4 conjunctions there are $3 \times 20 = 60$ years,
between 5 conjunctions there are $4 \times 20 = 80$ years and so forth.

By continuing in this way, we reach the number of 41 conjunctions, where $40 \times 20 = 800$ years must fall between. A journey through 5 instead of 4 elements would embrace the period of 800 years increased by a further interval of 200 years, i.e. a time interval of 1000 years. Now it is easy to calcultate that we need exactly 51 conjunctions to embrace a period of 1000 years, i.e. there stands in the beginning and at the end of a period of 1000 years one Jupiter/Saturn-conjunction. Herein lies the solution of the problem raised by Kālīcaraṇa: The number 1000 of the 1000-petalled lotus is itself supposed to be the product of the alphabet repeated 20 times. How is it possible if the alphabet consists of 51 letters ? We know his solution (see page 35, footnote 36). Our own solution, on the other hand, is as follows: First of all, one should remember that Gichtel (see illustration 11) localizes the planets Jupiter and Saturn in the head. It is, therefore, hardly to be doubted that the number 1000 of the 1000-petalled lotus is to be traced back to the conjunctions of Jupiter and Saturn, especially as in both cases the number 1000 is composed of the factors 50 and 20. But we don't have to omit one of the 51 letters like Kālīcaraṇa who thinks it necessary to do so, in order to arrive at the number 1000, but on the contrary, we just *need* all the 51 letters (which, from gestalt-astronomical considerations) represent the 51 Jupiter-Saturn-conjunctions, in order to obtain exactly 50 intervals of 20 years each ! One can now put forth the following consideration: The first conjunction introduces the first 20 years interval which ends just *before* conjunction 2. Thus conjunction 2 introduces the second 20 years interval which ends just before conjunction 3 and so on. Conjunction 50 introduces the 50th 20 years interval which ends before the 51st and last conjunction. That is the reason why the sequence of letters stops *before* the letter Kṣa, according to the cited text of Kālīcaraṇa. According to this interpretation based on Gestalt-Astronomy, in the 1000-petalled lotus, one need not, strictly speaking, deal with 1000 letters. *There are only* 51 *letters* and *out of them* result automatically 1000 years. Accordingly, every lotus-petal represents *one year* and not one letter (or one Jupiter/Saturn conjunction).[59] This may be the reason wherefore the original texts never talk of 20 × 50 letters. Also the text cited by Kālīcaraṇa does not do it.[60]

Only Kālīcaraṇa, and after him, Avalon speak expressly about the 20 × 50 letters which make up the 1000-petal-number of this lotus, which is quite right as, as a matter of fact, here 20 × 50 are dealt with—only in a somewhat different sense (as shown above) than Kālīcaraṇa has understood it. After the entire facts of the case are cleared up, one can, at the most, speak of the "1000 letters" in a not literal sense. Each petal stands for one year. As 20 years are counted respectively after each conjunction i.e., therefore, for each definite letter, 20 lotus-petals fall, so to speak, under one letter. Therefore 20 petals under the *a*, further 20 under the *ā*,...and finally the last 20 letters under *Lla*. In this way, we again agree with Kālīcaraṇa—indeed, only under the above-mentioned presuppositions.

Herewith the theme about the 1000-petalled lotus comes to an end. It is hardly necessary to point out that in the case of this lotus, what is dealt with, is evidently not a *gestalt*-number but distinctly a *period*-number.

As has already been mentioned, and as will be still demonstrated, the remaining 6 centres exhibit no period-numbers but the gestalt-numbers of the corresponding planets. Our task is, in

59 Otherwise, there would be 1000 conjunctions.

60 (1) *Ṣaṭ-cakra-nirūpaṇa*, verse 40 (about the 1000 petalled lotus): "Its body is luminous with the letters beginning with A and it is the absolute bliss" (*Serpent Power* p. 419).

(2) *Syāmā-Saparyā*: "The lotus Sahasrāra, downward turned in the head, is white. Its filaments are of the colour of the rising sun; all the letters of the alphabet are in its petals" (*Serpent Power* p. 496).

(3) *Bālā-Vilāsa* Tantra: "As you awake in the morning, meditate on your Guru in the white lotus of a thousand petals, the head of which great lotus is downward turned and which is decorated with all the letters of the Alphabet" (*Serpent Power*, p. 497). In the sequel, a reference is made in both the last texts to the triangle in the inner part of the lotus and the 51 letters.

the first place, concerned with the 6 centres. Only with the six first planets, Ptolemy connects the particular numbers and also the *Ṣaṭ-cakra-nirūpaṇa* is, according to its title, a description of 6 centres. But in reality the work deals with the 7th centre as well which, as we have already mentioned, is considered as a "potentiated summary" of the 6 other centres. In any way, it is worth while asserting that the astronomical consideration can be successfully implemented not only in the case of the 6 lower centres but also with respect to the last lotus.

We shall now pass on to describe the 20-years-cycle of Mercury.

Mercury

Just as earlier we discovered the temporal forms of the Moon, when we fixed the striking, spatially traceable appearances of the moon belonging together, and thought them connected with lines, we now seek to find out the striking temporal forms of the planets Mercury and Venus.

Now it is not to be doubted that the most striking phenomena of these planets are their *heliacian ascents*[61] and that from here the *conjunctions* preceding them and their localization in the Zodiac are bound to awaken the interest of a systematic observer of the sky. When we fix the positions of conjunctions of Mercury and Sun in the Zodiac and regard them as connected through lines, then there appears to us again a *trigon* (which, however, is much more regular than the Moon-Trigon). When we join to it the corresponding figure which arises through the *lower* conjunctions fixed previously in the Zodiac, there arises likewise a triangle, which, however, stands related to the preceding triangle as a reflected image (see illustration 15).

This hexagram forms itself in one year. But now this figure does not remain in rest. The heliacian ascents or the preceding conjunctions respectively do not always take place in the same place of the Zodiac but shift themselves in course of time. *For a full revolution in the Zodiac, the hexagram requires fairly exactly* 20 *years* ! Thus they are the 20 years of Mercury meant by Ptolemy. They have only a significance in their relation to the six-fold pattern of the Mercury-hexagram.

61 The heliacian ascent of a planet is its first appearance in the sky after a period of invisibility due to its conjunction with the Sun.

Illustration 15

Mercury-Hexagram. The sequence of individual conjunctions ensues in west-east direction. The hexagram as a whole travels in east-west direction.

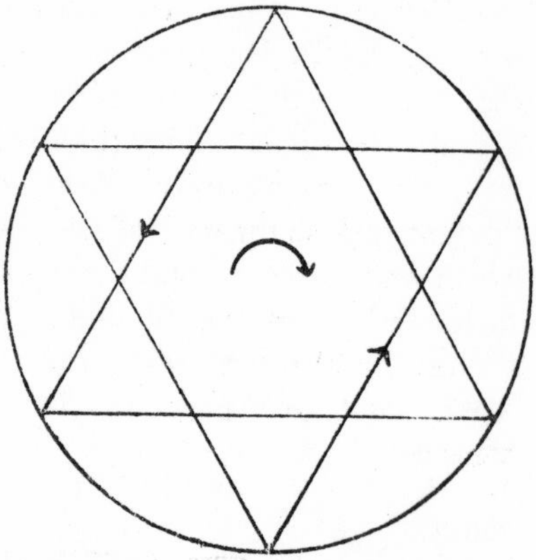

Like in the Yoga-system the centre 1, as the four-petalled flower, represents the four-fold temporal form of the Moon, so also the second centre, as the six-petalled flower, represents the six-fold temporal form of Mercury.

In this place, I would also like to draw attention to the *distribution of letters* in the two lowermost centres. In the *four-petalled lotus*, there occur *va, śa ṣa* and *sa*—a half-vowel and three sibilants. This number 4 is built up as 1+3, entirely corresponding to the structure of the four-fold Moon-pattern: 1 invisible phase+3 visible phases.

In the 6-petalled lotus occur *ba, bha, ma, ya, ra, la* i.e. 3 labials and 3 half-vowels. This composition corresponds to the structure of the Mercury-hexagram which is composed out of two triangles (3+3).

Venus

As in the case of Mercury, we fix the heliacian positions of ascent or the place of the conjunction of Venus in the Zodiac respectively; we also thereby consider the evening and the morning star as separate, which is in accordance with the nature of direct observation. The pattern of lines which arises through connecting the fixed points, gives us a double *pentagram* (see illustration 16).[62]

62 To my knowledge, the pentagram of Venus was, for the first time, rediscovered in modern European realm of culture by Dr. Martin Knapp, a lecturer of astronomy in his time, at the University of Basel. He published his discovery in an essay *Pentagramma Veneris*, Basel 1934.

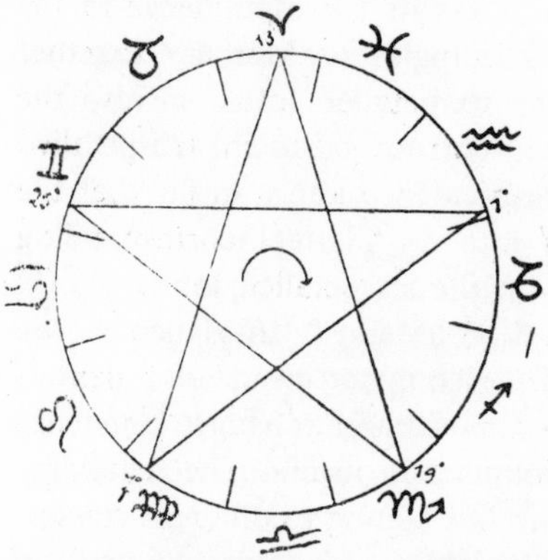

Illustration 16
Venus-Pentagram in the Zodiac

These two figures are not found, as was the case for the triangles of Mercury, to lie in the position of a reflected image in relation to one another, but they approximately cover each other. The distribution of the points of the pentagram in the 12-fold Zodiac always ensues such that either there are *two* points in the neighbouring *male* signs (they are the signs of Fire and Air) and three points in female signs (signs of Earth and Water), or in the reverse order: The three points stay in the neighbouring male signs and the two points in the neighbouring female signs. (See the synopsis on page 50).

Illustration 16 shows the geometrical necessity of the (3+2)-organization of the points of the pentagram which refer to the 12-fold Zodiac. The three uppermost points are found in Gemini, Aries and Aquarius (all male signs), the two lowermost in Virgo and Scorpio (both female signs). It is clear that the pentagram represents *in itself* a "pure five-ness" in which every point plays the same role, as it is at 72° distance from the neighbouring point—towards the left and towards the right. Only, the pentagram as *referred to the* 12-*fold Zodiac*, brings about a definite classification of points in two main groups. One main group contains 3, the other 2 parts. Between the signs of the Zodiac of one group, there is "friendship" (sextile), on the other hand, between the external signs of the Zodiac of the other *different* groups, there rules "enmity" (quadrature).[63]

63 See illustration 16. Gemini, Aries and Aquarius stand in harmony with one another, so also Virgo and Scorpio. On the other hand, Gemini and Virgo stand in the quadrature aspect, i.e. disharmoniously with one another, as also the zodiacal signs Aquarius and Scorpio.

Just as the square of the Moon has its correspondence in the four-petalled lotus and the two triangles of Mercury together have their correspondence in the six-petalled lotus, so also the two pentagrams of Venus together correspond to the ten-petalled lotus. Does here also the correspondence apply so far that the ten letters organize themselves into 5+5 letters, corresponding to the two pentagrams (just as in the six-petalled lotus, the six letters organize themselves into 3+3 letters) ? A glance at the 10-petalled lotus shows us first the compact group of 5 dentals *ta, tha, da, dha,* and *na* which we can interpret as a correspondence with the five-fold pentagram, compact in itself. The remaining five letters form no unitary group but belong to different classes: *ḍa, ṭha, ṇa* are cerebrals, *pa, pha* labials. We thus see a uniform group of 5 letters, while the remaining five are divided into 2+3.

One would allow this last differentiation to hold good only as a correspondence to the previously mentioned astronomical facts (the points of the pentagram in 2 male and 3 female or 2 female and 3 male signs respectively). On the other hand, without reference to the 12-fold Zodiac, no astronomical reality corresponds to the latter differentiation of letters in 2+3.

If we name the correspondence of the *total* number of lotus-petals with the *whole* pattern of the concerned planets a *correspondence of first order*, the correspondence of the next differentiation of lotus-petals (for example, the four-petalled in 3+1) to the corresponding differentiation within the planet-pattern (in this case, of Moon-pattern 1+3) would be a *correspondence of second order*. Also the differentiation of 6 into 3+3 in the six-petalled lotus on the one hand, and in the Mercury-pattern on the other, concerns a correspondence of second order, as does also that of 10 into 5+5. But the still more far-reaching differentiation within the 5 into 3+2, concerns a *correspondence of third order*. We would be able now to posit methodically the following rule: "With increasing order of correspondence, the *certainty* of the correspondence decreases."

As far as the correspondence of first order is concerned, there is nothing doubtful. The certainty of correspondence is 100%. But not everyone will acknowledge the correspondence of second order. Anyone could say: the distribution of letters in the four-petalled lotus into 1+3 corresponds only by chance to the differentiation into 1+3 in the Moon-pattern. And so also with reference to the other lotus-flowers. But now, as a matter of fact, *all* the lotus-flowers exhibit a correspondence of second order to the planets belonging to them. Then all this would be by chance only, which would be very improbable. But beyond this, some further investigations have been made, which, though it is not possible to mention them here, would be able to set aside completely every doubt about the reality of the correspondences of the second order. On the other hand, the correspondence of the third order, with reference to the ten-petalled lotus and the Venus-pattern is not yet confirmed from other investigations. One may take it provisionally as a reference to a possible connection.

Ptolemy sets the period-number 8 in the place of Venus. This is the timer-interval in which Venus marks a pentagram in the Zodiac. The 8 years of Venus[64] mentioned by Ptolemy and the 20 years of Mercury are only intelligible in their reference to the figures in the sky formed by these planets: the pentagram of Venus and the hexagram of Mercury. *That shows that the numbers of the age-periods of man mentioned by Ptolemy and the numbers of lotus-petals taught in the Yoga-system belong together.*

Sun-Moon and Sun-Jupiter

If we recall to our memory the gestalt-number of the Sun, which, referring to the Moon, amounts to 12, we can sum up and say, if we survey the first four lotus-flowers, that the primary gestalt-numbers of the planets Moon, Mercury, Venus and Sun are 4, 6, 10 and 12 in this sequence.

One could not have been able to connect other gestalt-numbers with Mercury, Venus and the Sun. On the other hand, the trigon as a second form could also, as we saw, be connected with the Moon. The gestalt-number 3 of the Moon is, for the observer of the heavens, of not less significance than the gestalt-number 6 and 10 of Mercury and Venus. But it is to be fundamentally distinguished from the other numbers (4 of the Moon, 6 of

64 As the hexagram does not remain in place but turns itself in the Zodiac, so also the double pentagram turns itself in the Zodiac. The interval which is required for the full revolution of the pentagram amounts roundly to 1250 years. While Ptolemy kept his Mercury-number at the basis of the interval of a full revolution of the hexagram, he took, as Venus-number, the time-interval in which the double pentagram forms itself once.

Mercury and 10 of Venus etc.), because all the figures belonging to here (square, hexagram, pentagram), have their starting-points directly in the spatially fixable conjunctions of *two* planets. On the other hand, the 3-fold pattern of the Moon, spatially considered, does not necessarily refer to a second planet but attains its connection with the Sun only in the time-dimension (through temporal fixation: the beginning of the year). (But, of course, it is not the *beginning* of the year but the *year itself* as time-interval.) As the cakra-system obviously has introduced the 4 and not the 3-number for the Moon, it remains, from the beginning to the end, uniform and consistent in its gestalt-astronomical structure.[65]

Supplement of 1976

A few years after this essay was written, I came across the book "Raja-Yoga" by Swami Vivekananda (Zurich, 1963). To my astonishment, the author repeatedly talks about the "triangular" lotus, instead of the 4-petalled one. I quote: "At the lower end of the hollow channel, there is what the yogins call the "Lotus of Kuṇḍalinī". They describe it as having a triangular shape..." (p. 52). In another passage, he deals with a breath exercise: "Thereby, think of the lowest Lotus, the one of triangular shape.." (p. 64). Or a page before that, again describing a certain exercise: "In this way you conduct the nervous current, as it were, down along the vertebral column and give a vigorous impulse to the last plexus, the lowest triangular lotus, which is the site of Kuṇḍalinī" On p. 59, Vivekananda deals with the "awakening of the coiled-up power in Mūlādhāra, called Kuṇḍalinī", which again shows the identity of the "triangular Lotus" with the Mūlādhāra-Cakra (as site of Kuṇḍalinī). In the same book, one can find also an illustration which shows the lowest centre as a combination of a 4-petalled flower with a triangle.)

With the Sun and the corresponding centre in man—the

65 In other contexts also the number 3 appears in connection with the Moon Already in the organization 1+3 of the phases of the Moon, the number 3 plays a role (cf. also in the 4-petalled lotus, the organization of the letters into 1+3: *va*+*śa*, *ṣa*, *sa*). And the number 3 appears as period-number in the 3 *years* which the Moon requires in order to form a trigon in the heavens, also in the 3 *days* in which the moon is invisible round about the new-moon phase.

Anāhata-Cakra (12-petalled lotus), we have not yet come to the end of our topic. First of all, we pass over to investigate the letters in this lotus. We find 5 gutturals (*ka*, *kha*, *ga*, *gha*, *ṅa*), 5 palatals (*ca*, *cha*, *ja*, *jha*, *ña*) and 2 cerebrals (*ṭa*, *ṭha*) i.e. $5+5+2=12$. Does this organization correspond with astronomical reality ? Here as already set forth, only two possibilities are in question. Only Sun-Jupiter and Sun-Moon lead to the gestalt-number 12. We shall first inquire into Sun-Jupiter.

Sun in conjunction with Jupiter

Here no subtle organization is discernible. Once in a year, Jupiter vanishes for some time from the heavens at night. The conjunction cannot be observed and thus, during a revolution of Jupiter, one conjunction is not different from every other. All conjunctions between the Sun and Jupiter are basically alike in their appearance in the sky.

Sun in opposition to Jupiter

Here an important point is to be ascertained. The most striking organisation, which results within the revolution of Jupiter, is a division into two: There are years in which Jupiter stands high above the horizon and thereby describes a great arch each day. When it has reached its highest place, it remains over the horizon, like the summer-Sun, for the inhabitants of middle-Europe for about two thirds of the 24 hours of the duration of the day and for only one third thereunder. Against that, there are years in which Jupiter describes a small arch over the horizon, and like the winter-Sun, remains above the horizon only for a third part of the 24 hours. Jupiter, therefore, stands 6 years north of the heavenly equator and 6 years to the south thereof. This twofold organization is distinctly perceptible; it results in $12=2\times 6$. But this does not correspond with the distribution of letters in the 12-petalled lotus. Moreover, the Sun does not stand in the foreground of observation but *Jupiter* primarily thrusts itself therein. The gestalt-number 12, divided into $6+6$, expresses here something about Jupiter, not about the Sun. Jupiter must stand in opposition to the Sun, in order to show this twofold organization to the maximum. In the conjunction it disappears. With the opposition is also connected the formation of the loops. In contrast to the Mars-loops (see later page 66ff.), these loops—every year brings one such loop—can hardly be recognized as such. Only a movement back and forth is distinctly noticeable. These loops are, therefore, extremely small and, although every year brings about another form of loop,[66] these forms are hardly to be distinguished from one another. In one Jupiter-revolution, 12 loops form themselves, regularly distributed over the Zodiac. Therefore, 12 here is the gestalt-number belonging to Jupiter.

We shall now inquire into the meeting of the Sun and the Moon. There is 12 times the Sun in conjunction or in opposition with the Moon respectively. When here the *Sun* stands in the centre of our consideration, a possible fate of the Sun immediately arises: to be eclipsed by the Moon. The astronomy teaches us that there are always two solar eclipses in one year. There can be up to 5 solar eclipses, but the minimum number is 2.

The position of these solar eclipses in the Zodiac is such that they lie opposite to one another and on both sides 5 conjunctions take place (see Illustration 17).

Solar eclipse in the ascending node of the Moon (Rāhu)

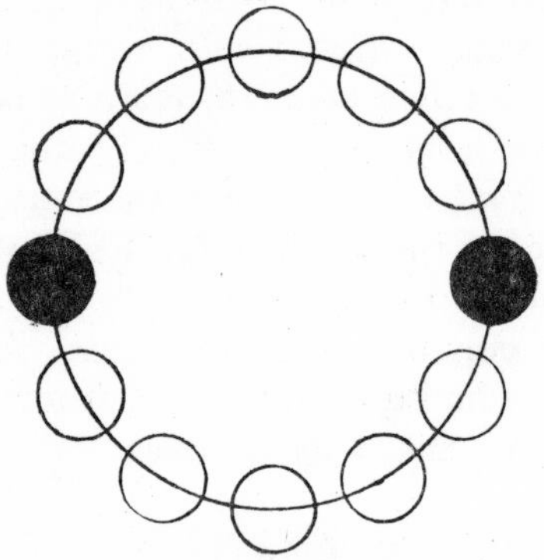

Solar eclipse in the descending node of the Moon (Ketu)

Illustration 17

The astronomical structure of the Sun-moon meetings is thus actually organized in $5+5+2=12$.[67] The distribution of letters in the 12-petalled lotus is the exact expression of this. The three possible solar eclipses are not considered in the

66 Only after 12 years approximately, the same forms of loop recur.

67 It hardly needs to be remarked that these kinds of numbers $5+5+2$ or $7+3+2$ have no more to do with periods but with spatially fixable events in the sky and are, therefore, gestalt-numbers.

organization of these letters. When we consider also these, a combination occurs as in illustration 18.

Thus one has, therefore, to consider that the 3 possible solar eclipses are always to be found next to the two "certain" ones; thus we get the figure in illustration 19.

It is perhaps not uninteresting to point out in this connection at the organization of our 12 ribs. As already known, the ribs envelop the heart and therewith the 12-petalled lotus.[68] Now the 7 first ribs in front are connected with the breast-bone. The 8th rib following thereafter has grown together with the 7th rib at its front end, the 9th with the 8th and the 10th with the 9th rib. These three lowermost ribs are, therefore, still below each

Illustration 18

7: number of the solar eclipses not occurring in case of Sun-Moon-conjunctions

3: number of solar eclipses possibly arising in the case of Sun-Moon-conjunctions

2: number of solar eclipses definitely arising in the Sun-Moon-conjunctions

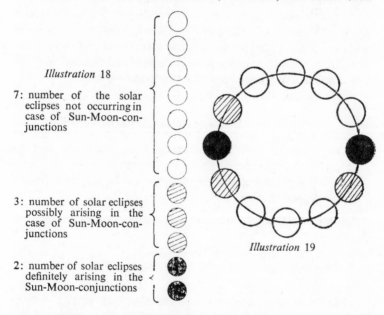

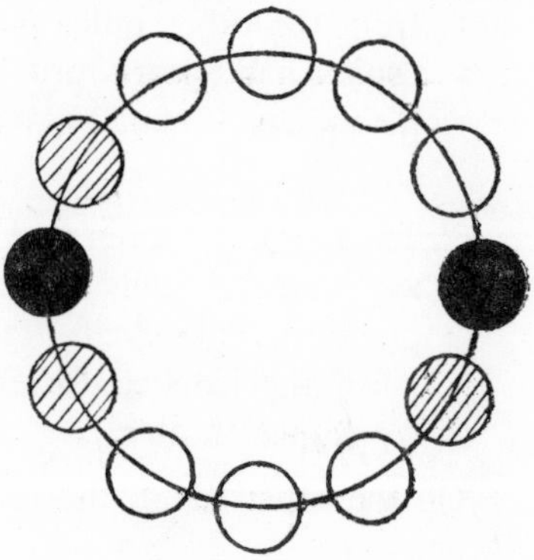

Illustration 19

other, but no more connected directly with the breast-bone. The 11th and 12th ribs are free-floating. Here again, as in the sky, the organization is 7+3+2. The distribution of the letters does not, as already shown, consider the 3 possible solar eclipses, therefore, the organization results automatically as 12=5+5+2.

Let us sum up: The inner structure of the rib-system and the structure of the astronomical phenomena correspond exactly,

68 cf. page 53f.

even in details. The grouping of the letters in the 12-petalled lotus shows also the structure of the same astronomical phenomenon, but not in such a differentiated manner as we can see it in the system of the ribs.

Mars

We now pass on to the 16-*petalled lotus.* The 16 vowels appear in 8 pairs: *a*, *ā* (short a, long a), *i*, *ī* etc. Gichtel puts Mars in this place, while Ptolemy mentions here the period-number 15. What takes place in 15 years in the case of Mars ? The answer is clear: Mars forms 8 loops within 15 years.[69] It is then, each time, in opposition to the sun and shines especially brightly. We know[70] that the Indians have been especially interested in the retrograde movement of Mars in its different phases. This is no wonder: Mars differentiates itself in this respect quite considerably from the other outer planets Jupiter and Saturn.

1. upiter and Saturn form *one loop once in a year.*
2. In the whole revolution Jupiter forms twelve loops, Saturn 30.
3. The loops of Jupiter and Saturn are hardly to be recognized as "loops". Only a movement back and forth can be practically observed. It is not, therefore, easy to distinguish the isolated forms of loops of Jupiter and Saturn from one another.

On the other hand, the following holds good in the case of Mars:

1. It forms a *loop only once in two years.*
2. *Only after one whole revolution*, Mars forms one loop.

69 In the Greek-English edition of Ptolemy's work by F. E. Robbins (London/Cambridge, Mass. 1956 Book IV, Chapter 10, p. 445), there is in the footnote the following observation about the period of planet Mars: "As Bouché-Leclercq remarks, why 15 years should be given as the period of Mars is a mystery. The synodic period of the planet is 780 days and its sidereal period is 687 days." One finds from this observation that the astronomical basis of period-number 15 is not generally known (i.e. no more and not yet).

70 For example, see G. Thibaut: *Astronomie, Astrologie und Mathematik*, Berlin, 1899, p. 27 & 66; p. 27: "Important attention appears to have been devoted to the different phases of the retrograde movement of planets, especially of Mars."

3. The loops of Mars appear clearly outstanding and are clearly recognized. The isolated characteristic forms of the loops can be clearly distinguished (see illustration 20).

It begins with the fact that Mars slows its movement and thereby increases considerably in brightness and size. Then follows a standstill (the end of the first phase) and thereafter a retrograde movement, whereby Mars attains its maximum amount of brightness and size. He is in the middle of its retrograde movement momentarily in its greatest proximity to the Earth. (The repetition of the greatest possible proximity to the earth ensues periodically in 15 years. At each loop, Mars stands the nearest to Earth at standstill. Of all the 8 possible loops, there is one, in which Mars is nearer to the Earth than in any other loop—this loop repeats itself with an interval of 15 years.) Then it slows itself down in its retrograde movement up to the time of standstill (the end of the second phase) after which the normal movement towards the right starts again. The gestalt-number of Mars thus is primarily 8 and not 16; but the distinctly visible *bipartition* in every formation of a loop, in which every phase ends with a standstill (i.e. it becomes stationary) (which is the first phase: the delay in forward-movement, then stand-still 1; then the second phase which is the actual retrograde movement with stand-still 2) seems to have found its expression in the division by pairs in short and long vowels. The last loop is approximately similar in its form to the first, as it takes place near the same place in the Zodiac, just as before 15 years. The 8 loops distribute themselves—not very regularly—over the whole Zodiac and thus form a 8-fold form. In every part, the above-named two phases are to be distinguished. We see, how the gestalt-number 8 or 8×2 respectively, comes to the period-number 15. When we consider the 16-petalled lotus, it is striking that the first vowel-pair (*a*, *ā*) as well as the last (*am*, *aḥ*) are a-sounds. This corresponds to the similarity of the first and last loop of Mars.

Supplement to the interpretation of the 16-*petalled lotus according to gestalt-astronomy* (Venus and Moon)

In connection with the 16-petalled lotus, for the sake of gaining a complete picture, the second astronomical proof of the

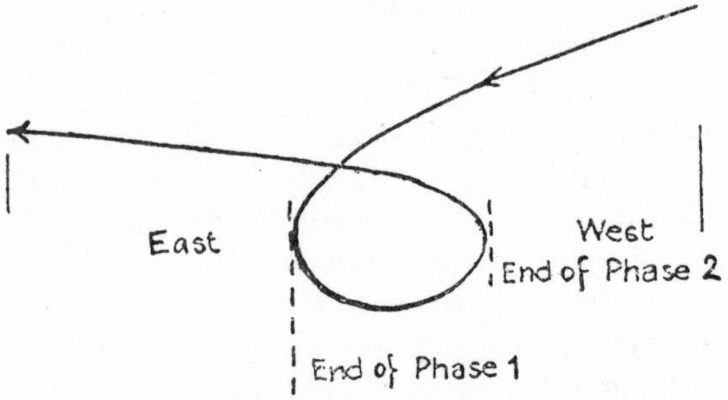

Illustration 20

16-number will have to be mentioned. As we shall see, it is directly connected with the first. Through the special sort of disposition of governances and exaltations in the Zodiac, the *Tetrabiblos* of Ptolemy makes this connection manifest.

Now where is another 8- or 16-number respectively in the heavens? Answer: Venus and Moon together form twice an 8-fold form. While Venus appears above the western horizon as the evening star and continually ascends higher and descends again after having attained the highest position, there are, in periodical divisions of time, Venus-Moon-conjunctions. In the course of the whole period of visibility of Venus as the evening star, Venus and Moon meet 8 times. After a short period of complete invisibility (3 to 14 days), Venus appears as the morning star, and again Venus and Moon meet 8 times. When Venus becomes again invisible, it remains away for some months (about 2½ months; see illustration 21.

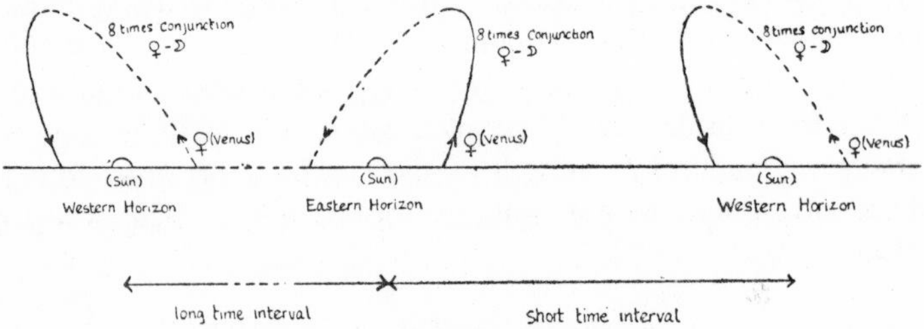

Illustration 21

Thus two pairs of 8 Venus-Moon-meetings arise. While the gestalt-number 16 formed by Mars is built out of 8×2, the gestalt-number 16 caused by Venus and Moon is composed out of 2×8. But the 16-petalled lotus shows also, besides the structure previously described (8×2), a clear organization (2×8), i.e. a bipartite of which the boundary is exactly formed by the back-bone. Both halves (see illustration 10) agree in the fact that they exhibit a-sounds (to the right *a* and *ā*, to the left *aṁ* and *aḥ*) on the above side, directly near the backbone; and the so-called *liquid sibilants* (to the right: ṛ and ṝ, to the left: *ḷ* and *ḹ*) on the lower side near the backbone.

For the ancient observer the impressive experience occurs as follows: During the first visibility-period of Venus, a Venus-Moon meeting takes place every month. The moon is there-through incorporated in another series of formations beyond its 4 phases: that of the Venus-Moon-conjunctions. The invisibility-period of the Moon following thereafter is so short that the moon cannot make *one* revolution without being "caught up" again by Venus, and become enrolled in the cycle of the morning star. Thus the twice 8 Venus-Moon-meetings are directly connected with one another to a 16-petalled flower-pattern whose one half unfolds itself in the morning and the other half in the evening sky.

But during the second invisibility-period Venus, the planet remains invisible so long that the Moon makes two revolutions alone. Therewith the Moon forms, in this period, only its 4-fold temporal form. The Moon is likewise "fallen down" from the 16-petalled lotus-stage and forms only the 4-petalled heavenly flower. This connection between the 4 and the 16-petalled lotus is distinctly to be understood in the cakra-diagrams (see illustrations 5 and 9). These two cakras have namely the same animal (an elephant) in the centre. Consider further that, according to the astrological tradition, Taurus (this is the Latin word for "bull") belongs to the larynx, and Scorpio to the sexual region. The two Zodiacal signs Taurus and Scorpio form, as is well known, *one axis*—a fact which is expressed clearly in the cakra-system through the relation between the 16- and the 4-petalled lotus. (Compare physiologically: the change or breaking of voice in puberty).[71]

71 One finds the *cosmic bull* in ancient India, expressing itself in *sound* (word, recitation, roaring, singing) and *sexuality*, described in details in the Groninger Dissertation of B. Essers: *Een oud-indisch symboliek van het geluid* (An ancient Indian symbolism of sound), Assen 1972, cf. p. 82 ff.

This consideration becomes complete, when we call to mind that in astrology (cf. e.g. in the *Tetrabiblos*) Mars is the governor or master of Scorpio, but in the countersign, in Taurus, Venus is the governor and the Moon is exalted. On the Taurus-Scorpio-axis, Venus and Moon are found on one side, Mars on the other, an arrangement which evidently depends on a purely gestalt-astronomical basis. Because *what Mars makes alone* as a "counterplay" (opposition) to the invisible Sun, *is accomplished by Venus and Moon together*, namely the formation of a 16-petalled celestial flower. This, of course, holds good in a purely formal way: there are two quite different "flowers" but both are "16-petalled" and both depend on the number 8.

When, therefore, Gichtel localizes *Mars* in the larynx while the customary astrological tradition puts here *Taurus* (and there-with the planets *Venus* and *Moon*) and when, furthermore, the Indian tradition sets in this place a 16-petalled flower, we have to do in all these cases with an exact representation of Gestalt-Astronomy.

Illustration 22

[Silver head of a bull from Mykene with 16-petalled rosette on the forehead

A head of a bull carved in silver, dug out in Mykene with a 16-petalled rosette on the forehead[72] (see illustration 22) is a further proof for the represented connections.

Illustration 23

Portrait of a Red Indian with 16-part-spiral in the region of throat.

Not less interesting is the title-picture of a book[73] written in Dutch (see illustration 23) which deals with the history of the Indians of Surinam in South America. The author by name Assid, himself a Red Indian from Surinam, refers to this picture by describing the herein represented Red Indian as a historical personality named "Kainema" ("blood-feud"). But he does not clarify in any words the still very strikingly marked spiral with the 16 rays. But it cannot be by chance that one such 16-rayed picture emerges in the region of the throat; besides, the *name* (blood-feud) is full of significance and implies something aggressive and outrageous. Moreover, the life-history

72 Published in: Erich Zehren *Das Testament der Sterne* (The Testament of the Stars), Berlin-Grunewald 1957.

73 Assid, *De eeuwige cirkel* (The Eternal Circle), The Hague 1946.

of the person represented confirms this. On him was laid the holy duty to revenge the violent death of his father in a bloody manner. Now Gichtel (see illustration 11) localizes the planet Mars in the same place of the body where also Kainema is strikingly marked. But as is well known, Mars also points to aggression, power and violence. Finally, when one reads the text on the 16-petalled lotus in the *Ṣaṭ-cakra-nirūpaṇa* (verse 31 A) where it is reported that the Yogi who rules this centre, will be able to move all the three worlds "in his anger", one sees how also here is pointed out the character of violence and power of this centre.

Jupiter

Now there remains only the 2-petalled lotus to be described: Gichtel (see illustration 11) localizes Jupiter and Saturn in the head.

First, we shall look into illustration 3 a/b. As can be observed in the illustrations and as has already been earlier mentioned, there is a 12-petalled secondary lotus between the 2-petalled and the 1000-petalled lotus. Involuntarily, one is rather inclined to connect the planet Jupiter with the 12-petalled secondary lotus than with the 2-petalled one. We shall soon see how this stands related.

We have described above how there is a clear bipartite organization within a Jupiter-cycle: 6 times opposition of Jupiter and Sun to the north of the equator, and 6 times opposition to the south of it. The gestalt-number of Jupiter in relation to the Sun, thus, consists of 6+6=12. In this context, Kālīcaraṇa's commentary on the first verse of *Pādukā-Pañcaka*[74] offers a significant explanation. It describes the 12-petalled lotus (Dvādaśārṇa) in connection with the 1000-petalled lotus:

> " "Dvādaśārṇa" is made up by Bahuvrīhi-Samāsa—that in which there are Dvādaśa (twelve) Arṇas (Letters). This lotus has, therefore, twelve petals, on which are the twelve letters. ...It is true, that the letters are not here specified, and there has been nothing said as to where they are placed; but the Guru-Gītā says that 'the letters Haṁ and Saḥ surround (that

74 *Pādukā Pañcaka*, in A. Avalon, *Serpent Power*, p. 483.

is, as petals) the Lotus', wherein the Guru should be meditated. This leads us to the conclusion that the letters Haṁ and Saḥ are repeated six times, thus making twelve, and so the number of petals becomes clearly twelve, as each petal contains one letter. This is a fit subject of consideration of the wise."

This quotation gives us forthwith a double clarification:

(1) We are informed that the 12 letters in the secondary lotus are divided into two equal groups—6-fold Haṁ and 6-fold Saḥ and, therefore, they show the same organization like the 12 Jupiter-Sun meetings ($12=6+6$).

(2) But here the number 2 is especially emphasised. In no other lotus except this, the same letters occur repeated. The fact, now, that here the letters Haṁ and Saḥ are dealt with, proves the connection with the 2-petalled lotus whose petals bear the letters Haṁ and Kṣaṁ.[75]

The 2-petalled and the 12-petalled flowers, therefore, show a certain mutual structure. But now the text mentions the identity of Haṁ with the Sun and of Kṣaṁ or Saḥ with the Moon. We have already seen that Jupiter-Sun as well as Sun-Moon lead to the gestalt-number 12. A relationship with the 12-petalled lotus in the heart should properly proceed from it. As a matter of fact, in the Yoga-tradition of the East, generally the place between the eyes is comprehended as a sort of "heart" of the head. It is clearly stated, for example, in the Taj J Gin Hua Dsun Dschi:[76] "The work of the circulation of light depends entirely on the recurrent movement, that one gathers the thoughts (the place of heavenly consciousness, the heavenly heart)." This heavenly heart[77] lies between the *Sun and the Moon, i.e. between both eyes.*[78] Further this centre has been named as the "centre of the void",[79] while the *Ṣaṭ-cakra-nirūpaṇa* describes it as "the

75 That the pair of letters *Haṁ-Kṣaṁ* is directly related with the pair *Haṁ-Saḥ* is repeatedly the meaning of the Indian texts.

76 Translation from Chinese by Richard Wilhelm in *Das Geheimnis der goldenen Blüte* (The secret of the golden blossom), a Chinese book of Life, Zurich 1957. The text goes back to the utterances of Lu Yen (born 755 A.D.), an adept in Taoism.

77 cf. also stanza 48 from *Saundarylaharī* (traditionally attributed to Śaṅkarācārya) in the edition of Norman Brown, Cambridge, Mass. 1958.

78 emphasized by me.

79 from *Das Geheimnis der goldenen Blüte*, p. 105.

house which is suspended without supports."[80] In this centre, the yogi carries out most intensively his withdrawal from the external world, he breaks all connection with it. Just as the "fleshy heart"[81] is the centre of the external world, so also the "heavenly heart" is the centre of the inner world, which becomes conscious through meditation and concentration. Only from the view-point of external reality, the yogi proceeds here into a "void", from the spiritual point of view, this centre is a "terrace of liveliness."[82]

From the *Ṣaṭ-cakra-nirūpaṇa*, it becomes clear that the 2-petalled lotus is the meeting-place of the Sun and the Moon, just as the 4-petalled and the 12-petalled lotuses were[83] already. "When the sun and the moon met at Mūlādhāra, that day is called Amāvāsyā (new moon day)...[84]

We should call to our mind that in the 4-petalled lotus, are found Liṅgam and Yoni—the male creative symbol and the female triangle. The two further places where a Liṅgam and Yoni are specified are the 12-petalled and the 2-petalled lotuses. In Avalon's book, we read:[85] "The three Liṅgas are in the Mūlādhāra, Anāhata, and Ājñā-Cakras respectively; for here at these three 'Knots' or Brahmagranthis the force of Māyā Śakti is in great strength. And this is a point at which each of the three groups of Tattvas associated with Fire, Sun and Moon converge.*

The three kinds of astronomical phenomena which result from the meetings of the Sun and the Moon are:

(1) The Sun-Moon meeting, related to a revolution of the Moon, produces four phases of the Moon (gestalt-number 4).

(2) The Sun-Moon meeting related to a revolution of the Sun

80 from Avalon, *Serpent Power*, verse 36 p. 404.

81 cf. *Das Geheimnis der goldenen Blüte*, p. 105.

82 Buddhistic formulation, *Das Geheimnis der goldenen Blüte*, p. 102.

83 That in the 4-petalled lotus, the *Moon* is especially emphasized and the *Sun* in the heart, is learnt from Avalon *Serpent Power*, p. 198. "...the 'sun' and the 'moon'—that is, the Prāṇa and Apāna Vāyus. In V. 8 of the *Ṣaṭ-cakra-nirūpaṇa* it is said that the Prāṇa (which dwells in the heart) draws Apāna (which dwells in the Mūlādhāra), and Apāna draws Prāṇa..." (The connection between the *Moon* and the *sibilants* is once again exhibited through the connection: *Moon-Kṣa* in the 2-petalled lotus).

84 Avalon, *Serpent Power*, p. 234.

85 Avalon, *Serpent Power*, p. 126.

*Obviously, here is an erratum in the text of Avalon. Compare : Avalon, p. 145 where these 3 "knots" carry the names : Brahma-, Viṣṇu and Rudra-granthis.

produces 12 times a conjunction or opposition respectively between Sun and Moon (gestalt-number 12).

(3) The conjunctions of Sun and Moon related to one revolution of the Sun produces 2 solar eclipses, occurring with certainty (gestalt-number 2).

Accordingly, one can consider the 2-petalled lotus as a repetition of the 12-petalled lotus (Anāhata) out of which, however, especially the 2 solar eclipses (and with it the nodes of the Moon, Rāhu and Ketu) are stressed. This is, perhaps, also the astronomical correspondence to the idea "centre of the void".

We come to the conclusion that the planets Sun and Moon each time are sufficient for the astronomical proof of the number of petals in the 4-petalled, 12-petalled and 2-petalled lotuses. Only the express mention of a 12-petalled secondary lotus above the 2-petalled lotus with the organization of numbers 6+6, points, unambiguously, to the astronomical participation of the planet Jupiter, which planet is noticed likewise in this place in the system of Gichtel.

We have already spoken about the 1000-*petalled lotus.* We saw in which way the planet *Saturn* participates in the composition of the number 1000. The 1000-petalled lotus is the only one which does not express a gestalt-number but a period-number.

The number 1000 in the highest place is a very old motif in India. We meet it already in the *Saundaryalaharī*, but we can also point to the already mentioned dissertation of B. Essers, in which he reproduces among others the text from the *Ṛgveda Saṁhitā* which speaks of the cosmic cow. This cosmic cow is identical with the *sacred primordial speech* and is, at the same time, described as *primordial being out of which all things are created.* It is further said of the cosmic cow that it is "*sahasrākaśra*", i.e. "thousand-limbed" and of "thousand parts"[86] is in the "highest heaven". On page 86 of his book the *seven ways of appearance* of this cosmic cow are spoken of.

Herewith, the configurative Gestalt-Astronomy, so far as it has found its expression in the system of the seven lotus-flowers, is almost completely dealt with. In order to preserve the main line in this section, many isolated problems which will not have escaped the attentive reader, have been set aside.

In another essay, I hope to go more into details of a number of extraordinary phenomena in the same context, for which this study may give the necessary basis.

86 Translation by B. Essers.

PARMENIDES AND THE TĀNTRIC YOGA

The following dissertation* attempts to correlate the Tāntric Yoga with the teachings of a thinker who is counted as one among the earliest founders of Western Philosophy : the Eleatic Parmenides.

Among the different interpretations of Parmenides, I select the one which has got the widest dissemination and bring out its characteristics in their most important features in the first part of this essay. In doing so, I rely, *inter alia*, on the lectures of J. H. M. M. Loenen[1] to which I listened in the University of Leiden between 1956-1959, as also on Dutch authors like A. J. de Sopper[2] and P. Hoenen[3] and further on the well-known dissertations of Wilhelm Capelle[4] and Wilhelm Nestle.[5]

In the second part, there follows a description of the cosmological and philosophical doctrines of the Tāntric Yoga. In the third part, this Yoga as a doctrine and as an empirical process is considered *vis-à-vis* the doctrinal poem of Parmenides; such treatment has double advantage; on the one hand, the details of the Tāntric system appear more in their profile, while, on the other, as I believe, a new light is thrown on Parmenides and his doctrine. I hold the view that Parmenides has been misunderstood with regard to the true significances of his utterances—a misunderstanding which has indeed turned out to be extremely fruitful in the history of Western philosophy. Because, until recent times, the way in which Parmenides thought, more exactly, as one believes that he has thought, has been considered as a compelling challenge to philosophical thought.

*This article appeared in German under the title "Parmenides' Auffahrt zum Licht und der Tantrische Yoga" in *Symbolon*: Year-book for Research into Symbols, Vol. VII, Basel 1971.

1 cf. J. H. M. M. Loenen, *Parmenides, Melissus, Gorgias—A Re-interpretation of Eleatic Philosophy* (Assen 1959).

2 A. J. de Sopper: *Wat is philosophie* ? (Haarlem 1954).

3 P. Hoenen S. J.: *Philosophie der anorganische Natuur*—(Nijmegen 1947).

4 W. Capelle: *Die Vorsokratiker* (Stuttgart 1963).

5 W. Nestle: *Die Vorsokratiker* (Stuttgart 1956).

I. Parmenides

(1) *The traditional interpretation*

According to the picture of the predecessors of Parmenides (the old Ionian natural philosophers) which Aristotle has delineated in his *Metaphysics*, those philosophers were convinced that there must be at basis of the infinite manifoldness of the ever-changing phenomena of the world, a unitary ground-principle ('arche') which is the eternal, unchangeable and indestructible ur-ground or source of all things. This origin also understood as a primordial stuff, a beginningless 'ur-substance' out of which everything originates and in which everything again vanishes, was, at the same time, the true reality, the true essence of things.

Now the 'arche' (the ground-principle) was comprehended by these philosophers individually from different perspectives and was, accordingly, defined differently. Thus Thales characterized the original (Ur-) substance as 'water'; Anaximenes, on the other hand, spoke of 'air', while Anaximander paraphrased the 'origin' with the idea of 'apeiron', suggesting, thereby, that the imperishable ur-ground of all things must be sought beyond the four traditional elements. Among all these natural philosophers at least the conviction was common that *out of nothing, nothing can arise*. We shall call this ascertained proposition the ground postulate of the old Ionian philosophers.

Now Parmenides caused a real revolution in the realm of thought because he answered the question concerning the unchangeable 'ur-ground', regarding the true essence of all things with the extremely plain and astonishingly simple sentence : "The Being is", (Literally : "The IS is". For special reason—which the reader will understand quite well in the course of our analysis—I shall avoid in general the term "existence" for "Being"). It is not that attempts have not been made to draw attention to the great outstanding character of this concise proposition. The ontological basic question, says de Sopper,[6] has been set forth by Parmenides as sharply as possible and has been answered by him as clearly as it was conceivable; he has anticipated the later *formal logic* which was founded by Aristotle and has applied it

[6] de Sopper, *op. cit.* p. 11 ff.

to his problem with ruthless consistency. We follow the dialectical process : "The Being is" : the unavoidable requirement of the principle of identity. But then there is *only* the Being. There cannot be the non-Being. "The non-Being is not"—which is the compelling requirement of the principle of contradiction. And thirdly, something is or is not—*tertium non datur* (there is no third), whereby the principle of *exclusi tertii* (excluded third) is formulated. Now, according to Parmenides, that 'something' is not anything, but it is the Being, the statement reads as follows : "Either the Being is or the Being is not. This can also be formulated as follows : "Either the Being is or the non-Being is." We have seen that according to Parmenides, the required decision turns out in favour of the exclusive recognition of the first statement.

Before we enter into the consequences of this logical triad, the epistemological postulate of Parmenides may be mentioned : "...the same namely is thinking as well as Being".[7] This formulation contains, as the neo-Thomist P. Hoenen[8] states, the basic proposition of 'the identity of intelligibility and reality', which proposition is also formulated as follows : "The 'ens' (being) is intelligible and the intelligible is "ens" (being).[9] In the Scholastics, this whole proposition is reproduced in the well-known thesis that "ens" (being) and "verum" (truth) are convertible : All *ens* is *verum*, all *verum* is ens.

We shall now summarize both the ground-pillars of the metaphysics of Parmenides :

1) The logical triad :
   a) The Being is
   b) The non-Being is not
   c) Either the Being is or the non-Being is—*tertium non datur* (there is no third).
2) The epistemological postulate : "The same is Thinking as well as Being".

[7] Parmenides, *Lehrgedicht* (Doctrinal poem), Fragm 3.

[8] Hoenen, *op. cit.* p. 17 ff.

[9] The technical term used by P. Hoenen is the Latin word "ens" for "being". The difference which in my opinion exists between the original "Being" of Parmenides and the "being" according to the later interpretations of the same word, I shall indicate by writing the "Being" of Parmenides with capital letter "B".

With regard to the latter proposition, Hoenen makes the remark that "indeed, from the view point of Parmenides, as it appears, intelligibility coincides with imaginary lucid imaginability". We shall return once more to this special view.

Now to the consequences of these basic statements. We shall investigate, one after another, the phenomena of becoming, of changeability, of origination and disappearance, of multiplicity, of difference, of divisibility and of movement.

Becoming—(a) Becoming is always the way to being. (An analogous example from the day-to-day realm is the following : to become white is always the way to be white). What already *is* can no more *become* (what is already white, can no more become white). Therefore, out of being no more being can become. (Out of being white, there can become no more white). Now every "something" when it is supposed to be *something* at all, is always *a being one*. When therefore, out of being, no more being can become, then out of being, too, no "something" can become. In other words, *out of being nothing can become.*

(b) When something could become, it must arise either out of being or out of non-being, i.e. out of nothing—*tertium non datur*. But the basic postulate of old Ionian natural philosophers ran thus : "Out of nothing, nothing can arise". Therefore arising out of non-being was thus rejected. Parmenides accepts and takes over this postulate and adds to it his own, so that it results in the following conclusion of great significance : *Neither out of nothing, nor out of being, can anything arise.*

But that is to say that *every* "becoming" is unthinkable. More than that, the consequent application of the epistemological basic postulate of Parmenides, according to which 'thinking' and 'being' are identical, leads to the inexorable conclusion : Every becoming, because it is *unthinkable*, is also impossible.

Changeability, Origination and Destruction

As every change in itself implies a becoming of something which did not exist before, every change is also unthinkable and therefore impossible. The same rule holds good for the phenomena of origination and destruction which can be traced back without exception to some kind of change i.e. to a becoming in regard to something. The origination of a thing always implies a simultaneous destruction of another and *vice versa.* Thus the being must be *uncreated* and therefore, *unchangeable.*

Multiplicity, difference and divisibility :

Now we follow mainly the statements of Hoenen.[10] Out of the statement viz.: "The Being is, the non-Being is not," there comes forth the compelling proposition that there can be only *one* Being. Because a second Being would be different from the first (at least from some point of view it must be *another* Being). But wherethrough is it different? Through the non-Being ? But this does not exist, so that accordingly, it would bring forth no difference. Or through the Being? But then it would agree with the first Being, instead of differentiating itself from it. And as a third possibility is eliminated, there can only be a sole, unitary existing entity; therefore there can neither be multiplicity nor difference.

Another possible objection may be briefly discussed; according to Hoenen and also according to Capelle,[11] the intelligibility claimed by Parmenides implies also an imaginary lucid perceptibility. The existing entity would be thereby a spatial thing, as it were, perceptible by the senses. But that which possesses a spatial extension is divisible. And thus the multiplicity could arise *through the division of the existent.* But this is not possible on account of two reasons : firstly, the division would presuppose the existence of non-Being, through which the parts would be separated. But as the non-Being does not exist, the origination of multiplicity through division is eliminated. Secondly, the division would bring with itself the becoming of parts. But there is no becoming, therefore no parts can originate. Thus is proved the impossibility of divisibility, multiplicity and difference.

Movement : Movement is a change of place and is therefore, like every change, impossible. Moreover, movement presupposes the existence of an *empty space*, as 'fullness" makes every movement impossible. But empty space is nonexistent. As it does not exist, there is no precondition for movement and consequently every movement is impossible.[12]

10 Cf. Hoenen, *op. cit.* p. 18 ff.

11 Cf. Capelle, *op. cit.* p. 159.

12 For the equation of the Being with fullness and of the non-Being with empty space of Melissos, Fragments 7/7.

In conclusion, I quote some judgements of scholars which summarize these discussions. Hoenen remarks : "That is the world-view of Parmenides : The Universe is solely one "ens", spatially extended and —probably on grounds of symmetry— globular and homogeneous, continuing, stiff, and unchanging and even immovable. A world of multiplicity and change is impossible.[13] And de Sopper writes : "The senses which reflect a changing world, in contradiction to this logic of Parmenides, tell a lie and deceive us. The world is not even a world of phenomena. It is solely a world of appearance. But even this is much too much : In fact, the world does not exist at all[14]". Before I conclude with quotations of Nestle, I will say, in brief, something about the reactions of Greek philosophers of the period after Parmenides, to this doctrine and mention the solutions offered by Democritus and Leucippus respectively (all this according to later interpretations).

The thought of Parmenides or rather the whole Eleatic thought had created a sharp antinomy which had to be bridged over. How was the outcome of Eleatic thought, recognized as absolutely cogent, to be reconciled with the evidence of the senses which appeared as not less convincing to the Greeks ? The new task was to rescue the world of phenomena. Of the different solutions offered at that time, I mention only that of Democritus.

K. Joël sees the connection between the Eleatics and the Atomists as follows : "He (Democritus) depends so much on Eleatic ontology, he follows it so faithfully with ruthless consistency that he at last can preserve the world as multiplicity and movement only through a break-neck leap in the negative.[15] This remark relates first to the fact that fundamentally was kept to the inner unchangeability of the *ens* and therewith to the comprehension that in reality, there could be no 'origination' and 'dissolution'. Now in order to justify the evidence of the senses, Democritus drops a basic postulate of Parmenides viz. the proposition that the *non-Being does not exist.* "The non-Being is not" says Parmenides. "Also the non-Being is" says now Democritus who, therewith, attains to the position that he can

[13] Hoenen, *op. cit.* p. 20.

[14] Sopper, *op. cit.* p. 13.

[15] K. Joël, *Geschichte der antiken Philosophie* (*History of Ancient Philosophy*) Tübingen 1921, p. 597.

just assume the existence of several, even numerically endless *entia* (beings, entities) which are separated from one another *through the non-being* wherethrough every *ens* gains its own form, size, position and arrangement. Now also movement is possible and through the mixing and the separating of the *entia*, all imaginable phenomena can form themselves. But for every *ens* in itself, there holds good everything what we previously represented as the Eleatic doctrine : Every *ens* is un-produced, therefore unchangeable, basically indivisible in itself, which last-named quality, as is well known, gave to the *ens* the name "atomos" ("atom", i.e. "indivisible"). (Thus also the *ens* of Parmenides— in this view — is nothing else than a single "atom"!).

We can now end this short excursus and return back once again to Parmenides. Researchers like Nestle and Capelle think over the doctrine of Parmenides basically in the same way as de Sopper and Hoenen. Nestle states : "In the presupposition self-evident to him that we have an organ in the reason (Logos, Fragm. 1, 36) which comprehends the nature of things, independent of our experience, Parmenides rejected with inexorable consistency not only the evidence of the senses but the whole world of phenomena and admitted only real existence to the Being which is recognized by and identical with Thinking (Fragment 5)".[16]

In another place, Nestle[17] speaks of "the complete negation of the phenomenal world" by Parmenides, "which he put instead of a proper elucidation of the same" and which "soon enough proved to be as untenable". We also read a further statement by Nestle :[18] "All life becomes numb here in the chilly abstraction of absolute being.—Completely unfruitful for the interpretation of the real world, this system is an instructive example of the fact that no philosophy can be founded on mere conceptual speculation under a complete desertion of experience and of observation of nature."

(2) *New Perspectives*

I myself cannot join in this judgement about Parmenides and

[16] Nestle, *op. cit.* p. 37.
[17] *op. cit.* p. 38.
[18] *Ibid.*

his doctrine. According to my view, Parmenides has not at all rejected the world of phenomena, its changeability, its origination and dissolution and he has never doubted its existence, either in logical or in philosophical respect. So, the second part of his doctrinal poem which deals at great length with the world of phenomena is not to be taken less seriously than the first part, which deals with the Being. The sharp radicalization and intellectualization of the ontological problem, as we have described it, stems, not from Parmenides himself, but from his interpreters beginning with *Zeno*. Capelle even goes so far as to omit without hesitation the second part of the doctrinal poem in his edition of the Pre-Socratics, as he is of the opinion that Parmenides here solely refers to views of his predecessors and his contemporaries and basically rejects them, so that these fragments "yield nothing at all about the own teaching of Parmenides and teach us hardly anything new for the remaining history of old philosophy".[19]

Nestle also shares this view unreservedly (which, however, does not seduce him to omit the second part in his translation). This is all the more strange, as already *Reinhardt* in his thought-provoking book *Parmenides und die Geschichte der griechischen Philosophie* (Parmenides and the history of Greek Philosophy) (1916) had stood up for a new assessment of the second part. Since then, there have been more researchers, who are convinced about the meaningful connection between both the Parts, eventhough, they otherwise, agree on the whole, with the conventional interpretation put on the teachings of Parmenides.

The subdivision of the doctrinal poem in two sections, of which the first deals with the "Being" and the absolute truth, and the second with the "appearance" and the "meanings of the mortals", has its exact correspondence in India in the doctrine of the two kinds or levels of knowledge of which, one is called the "higher" and the other the "lower" knowledge.[20] The "higher" knowledge (parā-vidyā) has the *Anubhava* (direct perception or inwardization of the highest Being) as the means of knowledge. The "lower knowledge" (aparā-vidyā) concerns itself with the world of phenomena and rests on all lower means

[19] Capelle, *op. cit.* p. 161.

[20] *Muṇḍaka-Upaniṣad* I First Half 4-6 by Paul Deussen, *Sechzig Upanishads des Veda* (Darmstadt 1963) p. 547.

of knowledge (sense-perception, logical inference, and divine revelation — the Vedas). This distinction, by Helmuth von Glasenapp called "the doctrine of the two levels of knowledge"[21] belongs to the basic constituents of Indian philosophy.

After what has been previously heard about the doctrine of Parmenides, it is not to be wondered at that its founder has been, in general, designated as the "father of logic" (E. Hoffmann) or as the "discoverer of abstract thought" (Loenen) and his doctrine is understood as "abstract monism" (Loenen). This image of Parmenides was also familiar to me until his doctrinal poem fell in my hand. Then surprisingly a fully unknown Parmenides emerged before me. He showed himself not as the thinker who, as it were, in his study contrived his tautological statement about "the being of the Being" but as one who, on the basis of a gradual change and increase of consciousness, arrives finally at an all embracing *experience of Being*, which far surpassed daily experiences. On the height of this overwhelming experience only is born the statement: 'The Being is'. Out of this comes forth a fully different perspective from what was known to us so long. We can, no more assume that Parmenides arrived at his famous doctrine solely on the ground of strong logical considerations. The 'Being' as a subject of logical or, purely speculative thought is, as it appears to me, to be distinguished from the "Being" as a result of direct Being-experience.

What induces me to understand Parmenides, in his doctrinal poem, as a *Yogin* rather than a *logician*, is for Nestle solely "the poetical form of a divine revelation revealed to him", in which Parmenides has clothed his knowledge of truth.[22] But this view, in my opinion, does not represent in this case the real state of things. *The doctrinal poem exhibits numerous characteristic features, which also characterize the Indian Yoga.* I even believe that this doctrinal poem represents, in this respect, a unique phenomenon in world literature : neither in old literature nor in new, have I met a text which shows in so concise a space such a great number of facts from the sphere of Yoga-philosophy in a proper right context.

[21] Cf. H. v. Glasenapp, *Der Stufenweg zum Göttlichen* (The Path of Steps to the Divine) (Baden-Baden 1948) p. 42.

[22] Nestle, *op. cit.* p. 37.

Now a last concluding look at Democritus. It seems strange when one reflects, where in the course of history of philosophy, the "Being' of Parmenides has made its way to. What in the case of Parmenides, is the final goal of his "ascent towards the imperishable Light" beyond the transitory world of phenomena and thus the expression of his illumination, is in the case of Democritus, the 'Being', parcelled out in an infinite number of particles, finally landed at the bottom of perishable reality ! The 'Being' of Parmenides and the 'being' of Democritus are diametrically opposed. But this is only because of the fact that the real or original Parmenides, and the Parmenides falsely understood in a later time, are diametrically opposed. The man who obviously prepared the way for what has become the customary comprehension of Parmenides was *Zeno* who is evidently rightly deemed "the founder of the dialectic" and thus must be considered as the originator of the exceedingly fruitful misunderstanding — mentioned in the beginning — with regard to Parmenides and his doctrine.

II. The Tāntric Yoga

The old doctrine of the basic correspondence between man and cosmos, which considers man as a 'microcosmos', and the cosmos as a Macro-anthropos "Macro-man", finds in the Tāntric Yoga, its theoretical expression as well as its practical application. Thus the relation of this correspondence holds good not only between the whole man and the total cosmos but also between the individual *parts* of man, and the whole cosmos, or the parts of the whole cosmos, respectively. The basic statement must, accordingly, read in its general form thus : The creation consists of parts which, in spite of their respective differences, reproduce or reflect the essential basic structure of the entire creation. Thus, this ground-structure can manifest itself in a more or less distinct and clear-cut form. One particular part may show only some main features, whereas other parts are more richly differentiated and more clear-cut. Such "parts of the whole" (*Ganzheitsteile*) are, therefore, at the same time understood as "partial wholes" (*Teilganzheiten*). The partial wholes chiefly claimed by the Tāntric Yoga in the sphere of man are the head, the throat and the trunk or torso. Here, 7 planes, in total, are distinguished, which have their correspondence in seven outer human regions. These are named 7 "Lokas" (worlds, regions, places of residence). (According to Woodroffe, the word "Loka" is interpreted as "that which is seen".[23] The "Lokas" in the sphere of man are named "Cakras" (=wheels, circles), besides the uppermost Loka which is found in the highest part of the great brain, and which is compared with a "thousand-petalled lotus" (sahasrāra padma). This lotus is never named as Cakra, while the 6 Cakras found below it are also respectively designated as "lotus-flowers". Every Cakra has a definite number of spokes (i.e. petals when they are comprehended as flowers).

[23] Woodroffe, *Serpent Power* p. 2. This etymology is traced to Satyānanda's commentary on *Īśa-Upaniṣad.* It is not accepted by Western scholars.

Thus the first wheel from below which is situated between the genitals and the anus — the so called Mūlādhāra-cakra — has four spokes. It is the region of the earth-element (pṛthivī). The second wheel from below which is found a little above the genitals — the Svādhiṣṭhāna Cakra — has 6 spokes. This is the place of the element water (ap). The third wheel — the Maṇipūra Cakra — is found in the region of the navel and has 10 spokes. To it is allotted the element fire (Agni). At the level of the heart, the anāhata-cakra is found as the fourth wheel with 12 spokes. The element air in motion (Vāyu) belongs to this place. These are the four Cakras in the region of the trunk, which together symbolize the same which the nethermost wheel with its four spokes as such represents : the world of the 4 Elements, i.e. the world of entanglement and involvement or arrest in Matter, for which the Western expression is 'sub-lunar Nature'.

In the region of the trunk, the two nethermost Cakras (=4= and =6=)[24] are understood together as one group. We name it Group I. So also the two above Cakras (=10= and =12=), we designate together as Group II. According to Tāntric interpretation, every one of these groups has a culmination-point, in which the Cakras, which belong to every group converge.[25] The culminating point of Group I lies in =4=, the corresponding point in Group II in =12=.

The throat is the bearer of the 5th element — ākāśa. This region is the Viśuddha Cakra. It has 16 spokes.

In the symbolic representations of the Cakras, a particular animal characterizes every Cakra in the centre : In the 1st Cakra (=4=) an elephant, in the 2nd Cakra (=6=) a Makara (a crocodile-like animal), in the 3rd Cakra (=10=) a ram, in the 4th Cakra (=12=) an antelope. These are the animals of the "dark" region of the four elements. In the 5th region of the throat (=16=) is seen again an elephant as in the nethermost Cakra (=4=). Only the elephant in the nethermost region is coloured and carries a red strip around its neck. The elephant in the upper region is, on the other hand, snow white and without

24 In this way, numbers marked (=4=, =6=) designate the corresponding Cakra, with its number of spokes.

25 Woodroffe, *op. cit.* p. 144. For the astronomical interpretation of these culminating points, see my *Understanding Archaic Astronomy* p. 34.

a band. Both elephants point to the principle of stability and security of the substances which they represent (below the "earth", above the "ether"). The earth-element, however, is found at the pole of heaviness and darkness (tamas). The ākāśa-element, on the other hand, is at the pole of lightness and light (sattva). While the "earth" represents a form of Prakṛti (=Ur-matter), restricted to a small space and condensed and darkened to the maximum, the ākāśa, on the other hand, is exactly the opposite of this earth aspect of Prakṛti—an omnipresent, most "un-densed" and light-radiating form of Prakṛti (the root kāś in the word ākāśa denotes "to light" or "to shine". Both the regions at the extremities are in rest, while the elements between — water, fire and (moving) air — are in everlasting movement. The region of the throat is named as 'the gate of the great freedom' (mahā-mokṣa-dvāram).

Before we consider the last two regions, we would indicate some further characteristics of the Cakras.

Every region is characterized by a particular sound which is specified in the form of a Devanāgarī letter in the centre of the Cakra. We will call it the "Central-Sound" of the Cakra. The spokes are also specified by a sound which we shall designate as "peripheral sounds". All these sounds end with a nasal ring—the so-called anusvāra, humming M-sound. This is represented by a point (bindu) placed over the individual Devanāgarī letter. In the transcription, this sound is specified by ṃ. (Sometimes also by ṁ). For example, the central sound in the 1st Cakra (=4=) is La. It is nasalised to Laṃ. In Illustration 1, the 6 Cakras are represented by their non-nasalised sounds. The total vowels are found in the region of the throat; the trunk on the other hand contains all consonants. Also from this grouping arises again distinctly the delimitation between the region of the 4 elements and that of the 5th element.

As it further becomes clear, all the four central sounds of the trunk : the semi-vowels Ya, Ra, Va and La : are modelled vocalically as peripheral sounds in the Cakra of the throat. They appear as the sounds I, Ṛ, U, Ḷ.[26] An exact analysis of

[26] According to the euphonistic rules of Sanskrit, a simple vowel changes itself before a dissimilar one in a corresponding semi-vowel; e.g. 'upari upari' changes itself in 'uparyupari'. So also the word 'manvantara' is made

Illustration 1

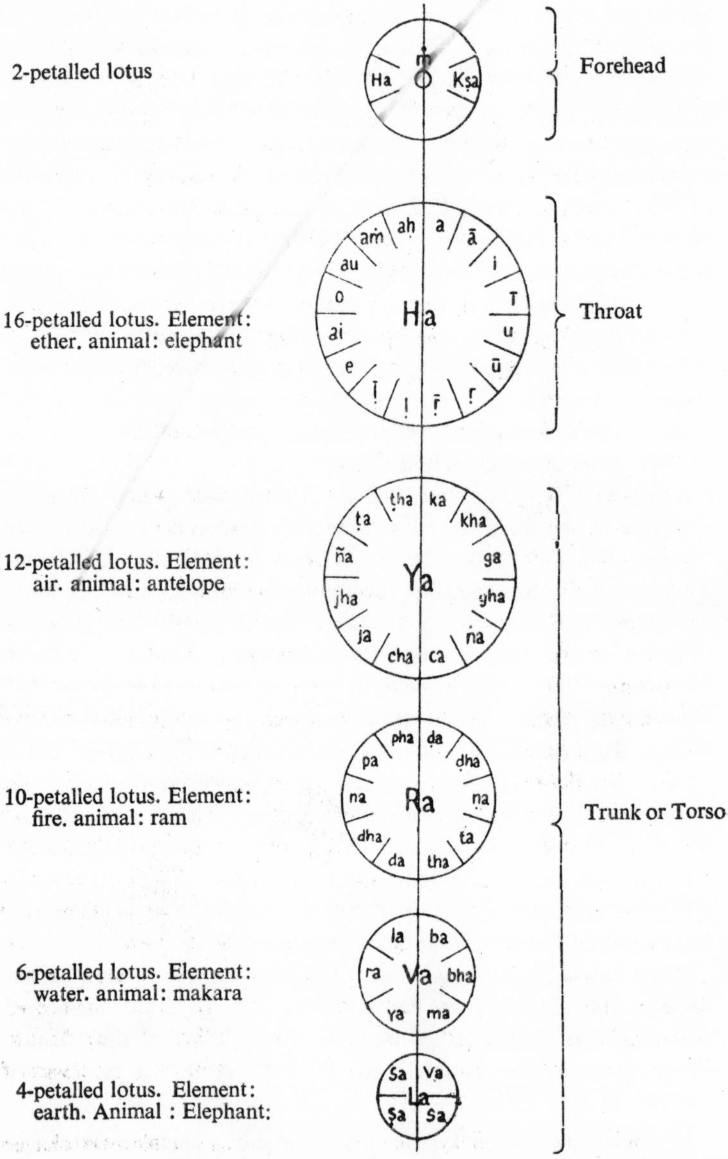

Survey of the distribution of letters on the lotus petals

the throat region, which we cannot fully describe here, shows that this region represents a higher world of light which contains the prototypes for the lower world of the four elements. The Viśuddha-Cakra is called Bhāratīsthāna (the dwelling place of the Goddess of Speech). This goddess is also called Vāk (word of God) and is designated as "the mother of the Veda". In this region, the word of God has appeared in his creation, a creation of course that has not yet tumbled into the darkness — an elevated creation of Light which has temporally preceded the latter dark and gross-material creation. We can now proceed to describe the remaining two regions.

The 6th wheel (Cakra) from below — the Ājñācakra — is found between the eyebrows. It has 2 spokes. No element is found here but the origin of all elements: *Ahaṁkāra* (the sense of I-ness), named[27] also the inner organ of action and the two thinking organs (*manas* and *buddhi*).

All the three organs together are also paraphrased in the Yoga with the word antaḥkaraṇa (inner organ). In the correspondence to the outer-human region, this centre represents the region of the creator beyond creation, of the divine thinker of ideas which have found their first pure realization in the world of the prototypes — in the region of the throat. The close connection between the throat- and eyebrows-Cakra is evident through the fact that the Central sound of the throat-Cakra, the Ha, appears as a peripheral sound of the eye-brows-Cakra and that as its right side. (In Illustration 1, to the left of the observer). This side is, besides, connected with the *sun* and with the *day*. The left side, on the other hand, carries the letter 'Kṣa' and is connected with the *moon* and the *night*. If we exactly listen to this sound, it results in the fact that herein Ka as well as the Ṣa are contained. But we find the *Ka* in the periphery of the uppermost trunk-cakra (=12=) and the Ṣ in the circumference of the lowest trunk-cakra (=4=), in which as for the rest all Sibilants are contained. Now =4= and =12= are also the bearers of the previously named 'points of culmination', so

up out of the words 'manu-antara'. The equation of sounds I and Y, U and V stems, therefore, form a living use of the language. That the liquid sibilants Ḷ and Ṛ are connected with the half vowels L and R, becomes directly evident.

[27] Cf. Garbe, *Sāṁkhya Philosophie*, p. 313.

that, we can discover in the sound 'Kṣa' the connection of the two Cakra groups I and II and therewith the whole trunk. Besides, if we consider the *direction of development* in which the Cakras have originated (in the original process of creation, these regions originate in the following sequence : =2=, =16=, =12=, =10=, =6=, =4=), we can say that the right i.e. the sun — or the day-side of the Ājñācakra is the origin of the region of the *throat*, while, on the other hand, the left — i.e. the moon- or night-side of this Cakra establishes the *trunk* region.

Also from here arises again the illuminating nature of the sun of the throat-region and the dark night-nature of the trunk-region. In the last-named region, it is not indeed fully dark : The moon appears here with its four phases, symbolizing the trunk-region with its four elements as a whole as also the four-limbed nethermost Cakra especially. The throat- and eyebrows-cakras form again their own independent group — we name it Group III —, the "culminating point" of which is found in the last-named centre.

In the region of the two-spoked eyebrows-Cakra, the origin of all polarities emerges into view : Day/night existence (Sat), non-existence (asat); knowledge (vidyā), ignorance (avidyā), consciousness (cit), unconsciousness (acit) etc. The central sound in the centre of the eyebrows is the famous Vedic Mantra 'Om'. It summarizes the orign of the divine, creative primordial word in one māntric syllable.[28] If we do not consider correspondence to the outerhuman realm but confine ourselves inside the micro-cosmos, here is the place where the human thinker, respectively the human 'I' rules as the creator of his thoughts, words and actions.

Finally, the highest centre, the 1000-petalled lotus is the divine region beyond the divine creator. When the latter is named Brahmā, the creator-god (thereby provided with the masculine gender), then, on the other hand, the 1000-petalled lotus refers to Brahman (neuter) which is also designated as Para-Brahman. This is in the divine sphere, the fullest existence and the most comprehensive consciousness, which is there. Its name is Śiva.

Now here a short clarification is necessary. The Indian Trinity of gods is generally known : Brahmā, the creator; Viṣṇu,

[28] The ideas "mantra" and "māntric" are clarified latter.

the preserver; Śiva, the destroyer. This Trinity occupies the level of the creator-god (i.e. of =2=), who is named here the "manifested God" also (in contrast to the Para-Brahman which is the not-manifested God) and is also designated as the personal God. The connection between Śiva the destroyer, inside the divine Trinity and the all-surpassing Śiva in the Tāntric sense is clear when one considers what "destruction" truly means. Destruction is only "destruction", seen from the point of view of the world. But it means basically the gradual regression of all existing entities into the Para-Brahman. At the end of this cosmic process, there is only again the Para-Brahman. But then the particular Being inside the divine Trinity which causes it must have a direct affinity in essence with the Para-Brahman — even, it must be essentially identical with it.

Out of this sphere of unconditioned divine existence and consciousness, (in the macrocosmic correspondence) with the aim of creation, Īśvara the creator-god also named Śabda-brahman, the word of god, emerges forth establishing in this way the level of the Ājñācakra. (Another name for Īśvara or Śabda-brahman is the already mentioned Brahmā. Also Viśvakarman and Prajāpati are the well-known appellations of God in his aspect as the creator of the universe). The creative word being spoken, the shining world of the prototypes i.e. the region of the Viśuddha-Cakra comes into being, out of which again — through a process of increasing black-out and veiling of the primordial light of Śiva — the four lower levels of creation (microcosmically the Cakras of the region of the trunk or torso) develop.

The Tāntrism teaches that Śiva is the infinite, immovable Being which has neither past nor future, as it is perennially persisting. The nature of this Being is highest consciousness and infinite light. In this Being, there is nothing "more" or "less", no impulse, no change of any kind. In short, we meet here the total characteristics of "the Being" of Parmenides. The state of consciousness, in which this highest "Being" is experienced, is the so-called *nirvikalpa samādhi.* It is the highest experience of which a man is capable. It is cognizable through the fact that it deals no more with an "object" of perception or thought which man "has", but with the highest possible "Being" that man *is.* Of this stage of consciousness, it is said that the knower (vedaka), knowledge (vidyā) and the known (vedya), coincide. "Śivo'ham"— 'I am Śiva'— sounds the formula in which this experience finds its expression. The highest Being, thus experienced, corresponds with the 1000-petalled lotus in man. But there is also another Samādhi-experience, the so-called "Savikalpa-Samādhi" in which God in his personal aspect is recognized as the highest possible object of supersensuous perception (para-pratyakṣa). Also on this stage, the Being is experienced but it is no more the full "Being" "without differentiation" (nir-vikalpa = without difference while Savikalpa = with difference) but a "restricted Being" which therefore leaves room for the genesis and existence of creation. (Strictly logically, a restricted Being is an impossibility but according to the Tāntric view, the logic of a particular sphere of experience depends on its particular means of knowledge).

One who is in "nirvikalpa-samādhi", is aware only of an unrestricted existence. And this awareness is unrestrictedly valid *for this stage of experience*. He who, on the other hand, perceives from the stage of savikalpa-samādhi has a twofold experience : Firstly, he has an overwhelming existential experience of Being, which is indeed of a lesser order than the corresponding experience of Being in nirvikalpa-samādhi; secondly, he views the origin of creation. This second level of existential experience corresponds with the region of the Ājñācakra. (In order not to lose the course of presentation in hand, I leave out of account the fact that there are still other regions, in the next compass of the Ājñācakra, which find their expression in certain secondary cakras and which establishes each just as much intermediate samādhi levels.)

These Yoga-experiences are, throughout, basically the same, but they can give rise to different philosophical interpretations and formulations. On the basis of the all-surpassing experience of Being in the nirvikalpa-samādhi, arose, for instance, the Advaita philosophy of Śaṅkara, according to which there is, fundamentally, only *one* highest Being, the Brahman and nothing else (a-dvaita = non-duality).

Still Śaṅkara did not neglect to mention that this holds good only for the highest mode of experience. He also accepted the Vedic doctrine of "two levels of truth" of which Helmuth von Glasenapp gives a remarkable presentation in his book on

Śaṅkara.[29] We have already mentioned (page 84) a division of knowledge (vidyā) into a "higher" (parā) and a "lower" (aparā) one in the *Muṇḍakopaniṣad.* Glasenapp describes the same doctrine in the form in which Nāgārjuna, a Buddhistic thinker, has developed it. In Nāgārjuna's work there is a description of "absolute truth" of the highest reality and "veiling of truth" by the world process, which holds good only so long as the highest knowledge has not been attained but which is, within these limits, of eminently practical significance.[30] Śaṅkara himself formulates, on this theme, the doctrine of the two standpoints (avasthā) of the explanation of the world. The "paramārtha-avasthā" is "the standpoint of the Highest Reality"; the "vyavahāra-avasthā" is the standpoint of the world-process.[31]

We shall now come to a central theme of the Tantra-teaching. If we posit the question as to where the ontological ground for the "world-process" and therewith for the "veiling of truth" is to be found, the answer to that question is not that Śiva is that ground because he is the unlimited, unmoving Being and can therefore, only be the basis of "absolute truth". Therefore, too, Śiva is not the creator of the cosmos but it is the *Śakti* who is considered to be the originator of the world. "Śakti" literally denotes "Force". She is the creative force of God (Śiva) and represents his female aspect. Though we read in the Śākta-texts, that the divine Śakti as the moving creative force of God creates innumerable worlds, while Śiva persists in his rest, remains unmoving, and absolutely inactive, still one may not forget that it is also simultaneously emphasised in those texts that Śiva and Śakti are fundamentally one. Śiva's creation and operation *is* what emerges into phenomena as his Śakti. A further central part of Tāntric cosmology is the doctrine of the basic principle on which the process of creation depends. This process of creation ensues, exactly considered, not through an (emerging out) emanation in the sense of an "extraversion" of the divine but rather the reverse : through a special kind of "introversion", through an act of variously differentiated con-

29 Glasenapp, *Der Stufenweg zum Göttlichen* (The Path of Steps to the Divine) (Baden-Baden 1948).

30 *Ibid.* p. 43.

31 *Ibid.* p. 66.

tracting and withdrawing on the part of the Divine. The gradual withdrawal-in-itself in a typical and creative manner of the divine element causes what, to us, appears as an origination and step-by-step emanation of creation. We have already said that the force or the power of God required for this act of creation is known under the name of Śakti. When God is comprehended from the perspective of Śakti, he is also called the *Māyā-Śakti.* Her specific activity, therefore, consists in the act of self-limitation, self-restriction or even the self-negation of God. There is also spoken of a gradual veiling or screening of the divine presence or an increasing darkening of the divine light. Now the idea of *Light* in Tāntric, as in general, in all mystic usage, is directly connected with *knowledge*, of true direct knowledge. Whether in the symbolic or the realistic sense, Light always makes something visible i.e. knowable. Where the divine Light is concerned, simultaneously the perfect divine Knowledge (Vidyā) is meant. The gradual darkening of divine primordial Light through the Māyā-śakti gives rise indispensably to 'avidyā' 'Ignorance'. On that account, the Māyā-śakti is also called the Avidyā-śakti. The Māyā as Avidyā-śakti thereby leads one away from the divine Light; she is the root of all matter and of bondage by and arrest in matter. But, as already stated, the Śakti, in the depth of her essence, is identical with Śiva and this fact operates in such a manner that in all created things, even in the grossest matter, a drive towards light, towards divine existence lies concealed. Sooner or later, this drive is noticeable in some form and then again it is the Śakti who appears forth, as a companion and guide leading towards the highest Light, towards the highest divine Knowledge. This aspect of the Śakti is designated as the Vidyā-śakti or Cit-śakti (cit=consciousness).

Thus, the Vidyā-śakti is able to lead back all beings again in to the divine sphere. In India, the worship of the Śakti but especially too, the Tāntric Yoga, depends on this doctrine. As the human body reproduces the total outerhuman region — not as an artificially devised imagery of analogy — but as a real microcosmic realization of a macrocosmic process, this body is also the field of activity for the strivings of the Yogi for emancipation (Mokṣa). The divine renunciation or withdrawal in respect of the original unlimited Being has taken place previously step by step. Every step or stage is the basis of a loka or cakra.

Every stage implies a self-constriction of the Vidyā-śakti and this is represented through a spiral line, the radii of whose circles diminish from above towards below. This becomes explicit in the diminishing of the number of spokes of the Cakras : =16=, =12=, =10=, =6=, =4=. On every stage, the self-constricting Śakti assumes a new form of appearance, a particular "Śakti-pattern" corresponding to the special nature of this stage. When it is said that every step has a goddess governing it (a goddess also designated as 'queen', or as the "gatekeeper" of this very stage), this is concerned with the particular manifestation of the Śakti on that stage. Although the Śakti continues its self-delimitation, there still remains back on the stage forsaken by her, a stamp or an impression of this stage corresponding to the special form of appearance of the Śakti belonging to this stage as an operating force. This is expressed in the central sound of this step : as Oṃ in =2=, as Haṃ in =16=, Yaṃ in =12=, Raṃ in =10=, Vaṃ in =6= and La ṃ in =4=. These are, therefore, different sounds, all of which, however, end in the *same* nasal-vibrating Ṃ-sound. Herein Śiva reveals himself, remaining ever the same, the correlate of consciousness of every stage. Although the principle of the oneness and the indivisibility of Śiva *vis-à-vis* the plurality and the differentiation of Śakti is basically emphasised, still with every "Śakti-pattern", there comes into being another perspective under which Śiva can be experienced. Out of this ground, the "indivisible Śiva" (niṣkala Śiva) of the highest region of the 1000-petalled lotus shows himself on every lower stage in another form of appearance. This Śiva-appearance is here designated in the point (Bindu) which causes the nasal sound in the respective lotuses and is considered as a manifestation of "Sakala Śiva (=Śiva with parts) i.e. of the creator-god.

Now, there are still the peripheral sounds in the compass of the Carkra and with them as many Śaktis. They all participate in the total constitution of the concerned regions. The letters are concerned microcosmically with certain physiological and vital functions of the body. That is to say, the same force or power (Śakti), which embodies itself in a definite sound, has also created definite bodily functions.

At this place, the idea of the "mantra" can be elucidated in brief. God as creator, is frequently named "Śabda-Brahman" i.e. "Sound-Brahman" or "Vāk": the creative word of God which is identical with the Śakti of Śiva. The divine speech is, in contrast to our daily profane speech, a process of great efficacy and might or power. Out of it, the creation proceeds. The "words" of God, which ripen into direct operation are the first Mantras (words of power) which have been uttered. The human being who in the Tāntric sense is designated as "the image and parable of god", has basically the same capacity or faculty as his divine father. He can also utter Mantras and therewith create worlds. Indeed for that purpose he must first be a real "man". But today's man is, throughout, still as "Paśu" "a bound animal". He can, therefore, neither *think* like man nor *speak*. The whole Tāntric Sādhana ("the way of practice") is now directed to actualize the potential man into a real man. The human action, speech, and thought is purified and changed through the ritual and later through the gradual steps of the Yoga. In the context of this training of mind and spirit, the Mantra-vidyā (the science of Mantra) has originated. It depends originally on revelation (Śruti), but it has been confirmed through actual practice for thousands of years.

We now turn back to the body: Like the total universe, the body is a visible form of Mantra which is composed of numerous partial Mantras (Śaktis). This concealed background of the body now appears in the system of the Cakras with its sounds. The Sanskrit alphabet has been fixed in certain parts of the body not purely arbitrarily but rather the reverse is the case: The Sanskrit alphabet is in the deeper sense, the true essence of the body— this holds good for the microcosmic as well as the macrocosmic body— and can also be brought again out of this body. The test for the rightness of this interpretation lies in the fact that through the particular sound māntrically uttered, the Cakra, which forms the proper home of this sound and the functions connected with it, are stimulated in a local ascertainable way. In order to be able to utter mantras, it is not enough only to pronounce the corresponding Mantra but it is necessary to awaken the corresponding Mantra-caitanya— the Mantra-consciousness. Years or even decades may elapse without attaining the mantra-caitanya, in spite of practice. Among some individuals again, it occurs comparatively quickly, and in rare cases, an individual is born obviously endowed with this faculty. One day, it may emerge into view all of a sudden, unexpectedly, with or without practice. In this connection, it must be said, that there are weaker or stronger degrees of Mantra-caitanya. He, who, disposes of a little degree of mantra-caitanya can increase this faculty through intensive practice. In some cases, a pronounced special faculty can manifest itself in the nether stages; then the Sādhaka has the power only over a particular sphere.

Now, in conclusion, a word about the animals which are represented in every Cakra. They are designated as the Vāhana (vehicle or bearer) of the Śakti, ruling over this Cakra, who is embodied in the Bīja-mantra ("seed-mantra", monosyllabic Mantra), the central sound of this region. Every Bīja-mantra has such a vehicle, except the Mantra 'Oṃ' in =2=. This is connected with the fact that the Ājñācakra (=2=) lies beyond the region of 5 elements which are characterized in their peculiarity through the respective existing animals.

After the earth-element is created as the last one, the process of self-restriction comes to an end. A stage is reached, in which the Vidyā-śakti is narrowed to the maximum and her power of consciousness is so much reduced that finally she is represented as *sleeping*. In the form of a serpent (spiral), she rests rolled together in 3½ coils in the nethermost Cakra-region. She is, therefore, also called Kuṇḍalinī-Śakti (Kuṇḍalinī = rolled together). The macro-cosmos has its Kuṇḍalinī-śakti; as well as every man has a separate one. The inactive existence i.e. the sleeping condition of this Kuṇḍalinī is the precondition for the fact that man can maintain his normal consciousness in the world of gross matter. The usual daily consciousness is called in Sanskrit 'Jāgrat'. It is also the mission of the 'sleeping serpent', to render possible to man an individual consciousness. According to the Yoga-teaching, however, the acquired stage of consciousness is not the last one. Collectively as well as individually, the unfolding of higher grades of consciousness lies ahead. These grades of consciousness have a certain parallelism to the grades that have already preceded. Thus there is a Yoga-state which is comprehended as a stage parallel to Svapna (the dream-state) that points phylo- and ontogenetically to a past condition or state of consciousness. So also there is a still higher state of Yoga-consciousness which represents a stage parallel to the dreamless deep sleep (Suṣupti).

While, therefore, the man in dream-state has a *reduced* state of consciousness as against the usual wakeful state, the Yogin raises himself, in the corresponding parallel condition, to a state of consciousness *considerably superior* to the normal waking state. And the Yoga-state parallel to deep sleep is even still more luminous and clear. It borders directly on the savikalpa-samādhi.

After the Kuṇḍalinī-śakti has fulfilled her mission and man has gained an individual consciousness on the Jāgrat-plane, there appears a period in which she again will 'awake'. If this occurs, on account of some reasons, too early, it can have devastating consequences. Instead of carrying the man to the stage of heightened consciousness, it throws him back into an archaic state of consciousness.

From what has been said, it becomes evident that mere awakening of the Kuṇḍalinī-śakti alone is not enough. Comprehensive preliminary preparations of physical, mental and spiritual kind form the main constituent parts of the Tāntric Yoga (called also in this context as Kuṇḍalinī-yoga).

The nethermost cakra (=4=) is the starting place for a great number of "Nāḍīs". These are channels of fine subtle matter or paths for the forces of life (Prāṇas) which course through the whole body. Three Nāḍīs are of central importance:

The Suṣumnā-Nāḍī is the most important of them all. It courses as a connecting channel of all Cakras inside the vertebral column, from the lowest centre up to the region of the 1000-petalled lotus. The Suṣumnā-nāḍī is further subdivided : In it are found the so-called Vajriṇī-nāḍī and within the latter, Citriṇī-nāḍī. As verse 2 of the *Ṣaṭ-cakra-nirūpaṇa* describes, in this latter nāḍī, the Cakras are directly fixed. The true nature of the Citriṇī-nāḍī is described as 'pure Intelligence' (Śuddha-bodhasvabhāva). The inside of this Nāḍī is named Brahma-nāḍī but it should not be regarded as a separate Nāḍī apart from the Citriṇī.

Left and right of the central Suṣumnā-nāḍī, there are the *Iḍā* and *Piṅgalā* which wind themselves around the *Suṣumnā* like two serpents. Suṣumnā, Iḍā and Piṅgalā, together with the Ājñācakra whose two spokes are often represented leaf-like, form together, as it were, the Caduceus of Hermes.[32] Iḍā is always represented

[32] cf. Woodroffe, *Serpent Power* p. 151.

on the left and Piṅgalā always on the right.[33] Iḍā is female and has the nature of the moon or the night. Piṅgalā is male and has the nature of the Sun or the day. From this is found the direct connection between Piṅgalā and the *right* side of the Ājñācakra (with letter Ha) and between Iḍā and the *left* side of the same Cakra (with the letter Kṣa). The nature of the Suṣumnā-Nāḍī is described as "fiery".

The central Suṣumnā-nāḍī (more precise, the Citriṇī which is found within it) is well known as the "royal way", because when the Kuṇḍalinī-śakti is awakened with the help of the methods of the Tāntric Yoga, she goes upwards, leading the consciousness of the Sādhaka (the Yoga-aspirant) along with her. If the Sādhaka is sufficiently prepared for this occurrence, then he is able to bear the ensuing tremendous widening of his consciousness.

[33] This refers to the heads—the origin of the serpents.

III. Characteristic signs of the Kuṇḍalinī-Yoga and the corresponding signs in the teaching of Parmenides

The basic experience in Yoga as well as in the case of Parmenides consists, first of all, in the fact that one travels a path leading *upwards*. Moreover, this is a path which leads, out of darkness, into the *Light*. The Sādhaka (the practising aspirant), thereby, feels himself carried upwards by an extra-ordinary force; he is relatively passive, as against this force.

From Dream-psychology, we know that our psychical powers, inclinations and impulses clothe themselves frequently in symbolic patterns which appear as persons (also animals) acting independently of us. Similar can be the experience in states other than the usual dream-state. The "I" of the Sādhaka then plays the role of Śiva who remains "inactive". Only the Śaktis are active. It is interesting to note that also in the doctrinal poem of Parmenides, as it were strictly in accordance with the rules of the Tāntric Yoga, the *female* persons have the guidance and actually they are always the active figures. Goddesses lead Parmenides on the way: maidens, who later exhibit themselves as solar maidens, point out the way. It is they who push back the "veils". At the "gate of the ways of day and night" the goddess Dike administers the keys. It is the maidens, again, who persuade the goddess Dike 'with soft words' to admit the thinker (Parmenides) through the door. Subsequently the maidens direct the chariot and the horses through the midst of the gate. After that, Parmenides is addressed by a goddess and instructed : She wishes to proclaim to him two-fold truth — once the full, complete truth but then also 'the apparent meanings of the mortals'. In the frame of this "apparent truth", which is presented in the second part of the poem, also the cosmogony, the process of creation is dealt with. The centre of this process is, again, the goddess who "directs everything" and stimulates 'luckless birth and copulation' everywhere. It is also a goddess who holds the Being in "the bonds of the limitation which encircles it". Therefore, by goddesses every event is led, acted, spoken and directed.

At that the principle underlying the goddess has two opposite functions in the doctrinal poem of Parmenides as well as in the Tantra-Yoga. Once it is a goddess who narrows and delimits the Being, which in the doctrinal poem of Parmenides is directly associated with the "origination and dissolution" which are "driven out far away in the distance" (and indeed this presentation is found in the *first* part of the poem ! Out of which results that the roots of origination and dissolution are traceable *in the realm of the Being itself* and it, thereby, again becomes clear that Parmenides does, by no means, deny the reality of origination and dissolution but merely assigns it a lesser degree of reality in proportion to the highest Being). This function which delimits Being and therethrough creates the world and pushes the living beings into their embodied existence is represented in the Tantra Yoga as we previously saw, through the activity of the Māyāśakti or Avidyā-śakti. On the other hand, the solar maidens and the instructing goddess lead Parmenides back again to the original Being. This is the activity of the Vidyā-śakti.

The Sanskrit word 'Āvaraṇa' means 'surrounding', 'encircling', 'limiting', 'screening', 'veiling' and is used to designate the activity of the Avidyā-śakti. When the doctrinal poem of Parmenides speaks of 'the limitations of mighty bands' (Frag. 8, 27) or of the "Bands of the Limitation which encircles the Being", we have here an exact correspondence to the Sanskrit word "Āvaraṇa", which is employed in the same connection.

The way of illumination explicitly consists not in creating the Being or the Light of truth but in throwing off the covers or the veils which have been created through the activity of the Avidyā-śakti. This occurs through the efficacy of the Vidyā-śakti and according to Parmenides, through the solar maidens.

The doctrinal poem of Parmenides indicates some problems which, until today, have never been elucidated satisfactorily, but which can be solved in the light of the Indian Yoga-experience. For example, the goddess in the second part of the doctrinal poem, introduces the cosmogony, the doctrine about the process of the origination of the world with these words: "Therewith I conclude to thee my reliable speech and thought about the truth. But from here, learn to be acquainted with the human apparent meanings by hearing the illusory order of my words. They have laid down their views in that way[34]....and then follows the cosmogony. It looks as if the world of origination and dissolution were created by men. As this is bad to assume, one has frequently assumed that Parmenides in the second part of his doctrinal poem wished to reproduce the philosophical views of his predecessors and contemporaries, in order to reject them as not corresponding with truth. But we have already remarked earlier that gradually, there is succeeding another interpretation according to which the second part essentially belongs to the whole poem and reproduces, indeed the cosmological views of Parmenides. I join in this interpretation. But still there is to clarify the mysterious speech of the Goddess according to which the process of creation would depend on the views of men. Gert Plamböck writes to this point : "Of course, men did not actually do so, but if they would be consistent, they would have to do it according to the words of the Goddess.[35] Plamböck (who shows, by the way, according to my idea, very particular understanding of Parmenides and his teaching in his short essay) cannot solve this problem entirely. It cannot be solved logically— it can only be understood through comparison with other mystic experiences. For that I again draw upon an Indian parallel. Exactly the same misunderstanding happens there.

According to an Indian formulation, Avidyā (non-knowledge or ignorance) is the origin of the world. We have already seen why this must be so. The "Being", God, is "Vidyā", is the "Knowledge". When God contracts or restricts himself, there arises the principle of "not-God" i.e. "not-Knowledge". This is only the basic structure underlying this double principle : God/Not-God (being/not being or knowledge/not knowledge). In reality, there are many steps or grades in the degree of the absence of God. There are spheres where God is fully present — as if there had never been the self-negation of God — and there are spheres where God, is present in a lesser degree, until to such spheres where God is absent to a maximum (but never entirely).

This Avidyā is, therefore, first of all, no subjective non-know-

[34] According to the translation of Diels/Kranz, in *Die Fragmente der Vorsokratiker* (The fragments from the pre-Socratics) (Hamburg 1963).

[35] *Ibid.* 'Introduction'.

ledge or ignorance but a cosmic reality which was already there *before* the man. Indeed, it is the ontological precondition for *human* ignorance — i.e. ignorance in respect of the true nature of things. One should reflect in this connection that, e.g. the discursive thought, the intellect, with which man attempts to master his worldly life, is considered in India as falling under "Avidyā". "Vidyā" is, therefore, the opposite of the same, what we commonly understand under 'knowledge'. 'Vidyā' is exclusively attained in the Illumination. When one has had this illumination once, and has experienced therethrough the highest knowledge, then one gains the impression that one has upto now grievously erred in respect of the true nature of creation. The creation, as it were, seen from "above" is now experienced as fully different as before. On that account, the creation, as it was comprehended from 'below', in the unilluminated condition of consciousness, is *now* understood as a product of the *own* Avidyā. One then feels that one-self is the originator of the earlier experienced creation. The Sādhaka sees the proof of this comprehension in the fact that the creation completely changed at the same time as the illumination occurs. Therefore, the cause of the former appearance of creation must have been *in him*. We see here, how a particular experience can lead to different philosophies. In his book about Śaṅkara, mentioned previously, H. v. Glasenapp describes two different doctrines. The one is the "Vivarta-vāda" (the "Illusion Theory"), probably first developed by the Vedāntic thinker Gauḍapāda under Buddhistic influence. I cite here the quotation from Glasenapp : "It is not the Brahman which changes itself into the world but it is we who change the Brahman into the world through our false knowledge. For that reason, there is in reality, not a "becoming another" or a change (vikāra, pariṇāma) of Brahman but a misjudgement (vivarta), a false comprehension of Brahman".[36]

The same experience, which lies at the basis of this Vivarta-doctrine, is expressed by Parmenides in the utterance of the Goddess quoted above. However, Parmenides as well as the adherents of this doctrine know very well, that this false knowledge (mithyā-jñāna or avidyā) doubtlessly found in man, is,

[36] Glasenapp, *op. cit.* p. 45.

however, not subject to the arbitrariness of man but is conditioned cosmically, i.e. is of outer- or prehuman origin and is to be overcome through the way of illumination only. Plamböck puts the facts of the case exceedingly well: "The men dwell in the house of the night; out of it, leads only divine entrancement. That means that the illusion meant here is not accidental but it essentially belongs to the existence of man, as he, in fact, is. The "meaning"[37] must originate and must last so long as man remains a nightly being and not allows himself to be seized by the breath of the Divine. This is, therefore, the special nature of the "meaning" and that is why it is worth knowing : it belongs as necessarily to man, as his eyes, his ears and his tongue" (cf. Fr. 7-3-5).[38]

In Tāntrism, in contrast to the Vivarta-vāda, the Pariṇāma-vāda is presented; according to it the creation has proceeded out of an actual, gradual change of Brahman. Indeed, all this happens exclusively in the Śakti-side of God. The Śiva-side of Brahman remains as before untouched or intact. Only from a particular standpoint God has negated himself gradually and thus created the world — seen from another standpoint, God himself has never changed and no change will ever happen in future. Precisely considered, the Vivarta-vāda and the Pariṇāma-vāda are no opposites. They are only different ways of looking ("darśanas") at the same theme.

We must still mention some further characteristics which concern Parmenides as well as the Tantra-Yogin. When the Kuṇḍalinī-serpent is awakened, an extraordinary force or power becomes free which courses on its path through the Citriṇīnāḍī. We have described the nature of the Citriṇī as "pure intelligence". This is evidently connected directly with the "intelligence" of the Kuṇḍalinī-power, which is continually emphasised in the Tāntric-Texts. As to Parmenides, they are the "much intelligent" horses (hippoi polyphrastoi) which emerge as the intelligent forces which carry the thinker upwards. But I wish to add forthwith that, though I see in "the much intelligent horses" a

37 Meant here is : The "human apparent meanings" on which the Goddess was speaking to Parmenides (see page 103).

38 *Die Fragmente der Vorsokratiker*, p. 41 (introduction by Gert Plamböck).

parallel to the intelligent Kuṇḍalinī-power.[39] I do not in this case, identify the two completely as the full equality of the metaphor is lacking here. (When I said in the beginning that numerous characteristics of the Tāntric Yoga-sphere are to be met with in Parmenides, exclusively exact parallels were referred to).

A further not exact parallel, consists between the *chariot* in which Paramenides is led upwards and the 'vāhana' or animal-vehicle in the separate Cakras. I draw a parallelism here, as a motive, akin to both, presents itself here but there is no complete correspondence. All other parallel motives dealt with till now, however, are fully identical. Especially pregnant, standing the test in many separate motives, is the *Śakti*-appearance and the *Vidyā-avidyā*-problem. In this respect, the doctrinal poem of Parmenides could have been the direct translation of an Indian Text. When the Kuṇḍalinī-śakti awakes and begins to course through the Citriṇī-Nāḍī thereby piercing the 6 Cakras (Ṣaṭ-cakra-bheda) the Yogin has a threefold experience.

1. He feels a glowing *heat* at the lower end of his vertebral column.

2. He hears a *sound.*

3. During the ascent through the Cakras, these make a *rotating movement.* But Parmenides[40] also exactly describes this and I do not hesitate to see here complete parallels. (The Greek word 'wheel', which Parmenides employs is connected etymologically directly with the Sanskrit word 'Cakra'). Further common characteristics are : 4. The already mentioned

[39] Already Xenophanes (fr. 2), the teacher of Parmenides in Elea, had made a corresponding comparison, when he described: "Then however better than the power or force of men and horses is yet our knowledge".

[40] The doctrinal poem begins with the following statements: (I quote here according to the well-known translation of Diels/Kranz). "The horses, which carry me hither carried me further, so far only as I wished, when the daimons (the goddesses) led and brought me on the widely famous path, which carries the man, who has got knowledge beyond all places of residence. I was carried thither on that way. There the "much intelligent" horses carried me (5) drawing the carriage and the maidens pointed out the way. The axis in the nave of the wheels gave rise to a whistling sound, growing hot (because it was driven on both sides from double whirling wheels), so often the sun-maidens, who previously left the house of the night, hurried, for safe conduct or escort towards Light, pushing back the veils from the heads with their hands."

maidens who accompany the ascent (Śaktis in the Cakras)— 5. The way, which Parmenides takes, is extolled as "much-famous"; more over, the way lies "outside the human path". This way is identical with the *royal way*, the Suṣumnā-nāḍī in Yoga, which also lies outside the usual sphere of human beings and which, nevertheless enjoys great renown. One gets absolute certainty in this respect only when one considers the whole context wherein this extraordinary way has its right place.— 6. To the *house of night* in Parmenides corresponds the region which is represented in Yoga as the region of the *trunk*.[41] —7. *The paths of day and night* in Parmenides are the Nāḍīs Piṅgalā and Iḍā which are not only named with the same denotations but which also play the same role as in Parmenides.— 8. The gate of the paths of day and night lies directly on the house of night and is named the 'ethereal'. Here come day and night together. The coming together of day and night is a necessary step on the way to the divine Being where there is no day nor night, no past nor future; in short, there is no Time. This door is identical with the *region of the throat* in Yoga. The signs are: (a) This region follows directly the region of the trunk. —(b) Here rules 'Ākāśa'= 'ether' the 5th element. (Among the Greeks the fifth element was also designated by Aristotle as 'ether'.—(c) It is the "Door of the *great freedom*" (see page. 89)—(d) The Yogi is able here to view together the past, the present and the future. It is said, among others, that he "sees here the 3 times" (tri-kāladarśī).[42] One must add that this is only possible because the paths of day and night— Piṅgala Nāḍī and Iḍa Nāḍī —are gathered together in the *middle* (Suṣumnā-Nāḍī); (out of the Suṣumnā-Nāḍī, Iḍā and Piṅgalā have once gone forth). With this a condition is attained, in which there is "neither day nor night", because "Suṣumnā devours the Time",[43] — 9. If the door is passed through, so in Yoga, the Ājñācakra (=2=) is reached, which, by the way — as we have already seen — represents the summit-point of the group, to which also the region of the throat belongs. The proper *source-point* of the paths of day and night lies here. Here also is the place where the Goddess, who teaches Parmenides

[41] One should always mind that simultaneously the *macrocosmic* correspondence is valid.

[42] *Ṣaṭ-cakra-nirūpaṇa*, verse 31.

[43] cf. *Serpent Power*, p. 229.

on the doctrine of Being and Non-Being receives him. *The whole doctrinal poem, is characteristic for this sphere,* is an exact representation of the truth comprehensible from this special level. The Being as well the creation are perceived here. The experience, which Parmenides had was not the highest experience of Being (nirvikalpa-sāmadhi) in the 1000-petalled lotus but the "restricted" experience of Being (savikalpa sāmadhi) in the region of the Ājñā Cakra. For that reason, Parmenides views a "restricted Being" although such an expression purely from the point of logic which he formulates, is contradictory. Therefore, a *speaking* goddess meets him here. In the 1000-petalled lotus, there is no longer scope for speech. Actually, the sound (Śabda) originates only *below* the 1000-petalled lotus. In the latter lotus, in the sphere of Niṣkala Śiva, there rules only Light.—10. On the way upwards, the Cakras are pierced micro-cosmically and, likewise, macrocosmically in which latter case they refer to the spheres of the planets.[44] Corresponding to it are the 'Lokas' which are crossed. So it is in Yoga. But also in Parmenides, there is found a corresponding hint, because it is said that the man "who has knowledge" (Parmenides) would be carried "beyond all abodes (places)". The Greek text here runs as following : "....*Kata pant astee*...." The translation : "..beyond all abodes (places)" originates from Diels/Kranz. On this passage, there has been much discussion and even today the discussion has not ended. Two other renderings of this passage show how little one knows what to make of it. Nestle, together with Karsten reads the passage[45] different from Diels/Kranz, namely : "....*Kata pant adaee*...." and translates ..."Which through darkness leads the man of knowledge to the goal". Capelle, on the other hand, with Meineke and Jaeger,[46] reads : "....*Kata pant asinee*...." and translates : Who "leads the man of knowledge intact to the goal". I keep to the text and the translation accepted by Diels/Kranz and interpret the "abodes" or "places", *astee,* as "*lokas*" which the Yogin (here Parmenides) passes through on his way. Thereby, the Yogī is first of all led *into* the "lokas" but only in order to leave them again and finally to leave them far behind (or "below" respectively).

[44] Compare the author's *Understanding Archaic Astronomy,* Part II.
[45] Cf. Nestle, *op. cit.* pp. 113 and 238.
[46] Cf. Capelle, *op. cit.* p. 163.

In conclusion, I would like to say a few words on the problem of matter:

According to the Tantra Cosmology, the world originated through a gradually increasing self-limitation of God. Every following step exhibits a *greater deficiency of Being* than the previous one : Therefore, the earth-element shows a greater deficiency of Being than the water-element, this again is greater deficiency of Being than the fire-element and so on. Now the earth-element forms the finale of total development. This means that here the renunciation of the full divine Existence or Being has reached the highest degree — the highest concentration. The divine non-Existence preponderates in the hardest stone in the highest measure. This consideration teaches us that in all matter i.e. in the total creation, the divine Existence or Being according to genetic steps is more or less present, but never completely absent. In other words, the non-Being is never absolutely realized or actualized. (With the words of Parmenides : "The non-Being is not.") From this point of view, all matter, finally *the* matter as such is defined through the fact that it is always composed of Being *and* non-Being. When we consider that the unlimited Being makes up the essence of Śiva, while the power of non-Being belongs to the Śakti-side, we understand the statement of the *Kula-cūḍāmaṇi-Tantra* (VII, 86), in which it is said :

'*Śivaśaktimayam sarvam yat kimcijjagatīgatam*'
Whatever comes into this world always consists
of Śiva and Śakti.

Exactly the same statement is made in the doctrinal poem of Parmenides with regard to the nature of the transitory creation; in Part II (Fragment 9) we read : "Everything is at the same time full of Light and lightless Night."

In my opinion, the teaching of Parmenides about the origin and the nature of matter completely agrees with the corresponding doctrine of Tāntric Cosmology. This can be confirmed to a still greater extent by a thoroughgoing analysis of some other Fragments. Unfortunately, this investigation cannot be carried out in this paper. Also, a series of other extremely interesting points of comparison between Parmenides and Tantra remains still undescribed in the frame-work of the present dissertation. A further continuation of our theme to which the present investigation furnishes the necessary fundamentals, is under preparation.

BIBLIOGRAPHY

ASSID : De eeuwige cirkel (The Eternal Circle), The Hague 1946.

AVALON, Arthur (Sir John Woodroffe) : The Serpent Power, new edition Madras 1958, first edition 1918.
Contains the translation of two works from Sanskrit :
1) Ṣaṭ-cakra-nirūpaṇa (Description of and Investigation into the six Bodily Centres).
2) Pādukā-Pañcaka (The Fivefold Footstool) Commented by Kālīcaraṇa.

BARAVALLE, Hermann von : Die Erscheinugen am Sternenhimmel (The Phenomena in the starry heavens), Lehrbuch der Astronomie zum Selbststudium und für den Unterricht, Dresden 1937.

BOHM, Werner : Chakras, Lebenskräfte und Bewusstseinszentren im Menschen, O. W. Barth Publication, München-Planegg 1953.

BOLL, Franz : Lectures in the winter-semester 1922/23 in "Kleine Schriften zur Sternkunde des Altertums" (Brief writings on the knowledge of the Stars of ancient times), Leipzig 1950.

—— : Ein Beitrag zur antiken Ethologie und zur Geschichte der Zahlen (A contribution to the antique Ethology and to the history of numbers).

BROWN, W. Norman : Edition, Translation and Presentation in Photographs of :
The Saundaryalaharī or Flood of Beauty
(author : Śaṅkarācārya), Cambridge, Mass. 1958.

CAPELLE, W. Die Vorsokratiker, Stuttgart 1963.

CUMONT, Franz : Die Mysterien des Mithra, German edition ed. by Georg Gehrich, Leipzig/Berlin 1923.

DIELS/KRANZ : Die Fragmente der Vorsokratiker (The fragments from the pre-Socratics), Hamburg 1963.

DEUSSEN, Paul : Muṇḍaka-Upaniṣad, I First Half 4-6, Sechzig Upanishads des Veda, Darmstadt 1963.

ESSERS, B. : Een outindisch symboliek van het geluid (An ancient Indian symbolism of sound), Assen 1972.

GARBE, Richard : Sāṁkhya Philosophie, H. Haessel Verlag, Leipzig 1917.

GICHTEL, Johann Georg : Theosophia Practica, 1st edition 1696 (pattern for illustration 11 from the French translation of Theosophia Practica (Bibliothèque Charconac, Paris 1897)).

GLASENAPP, Helmuth von : Der Stufenweg zum Göttlichen (The Path of Steps to the Divine), Baden-Baden 1948.

GOVINDA : Grundlagen tibetischer Mystik (Basic principles of Tibetan Mysticism), Zürich 1956.

GUNDEL, Wilhelm : Sternglaube, Sternreligion und Sternorakel (Belief in stars, Religion of Stars and the Oracle of Stars), Heidelberg 1959.

HANSEN, Wilhelm : Die Entwicklung des kindlichen Weltbildes, 3rd edition, München 1952.

HOENEN, P. S. J. : Philosophie der anorganische Natuur, Nijmegen 1947.

HOFSTÄTTER, P. R. : Psychologie (Fischer Lexikon), Frankfurt/Main 1957.

JOËL, K. : Geschichte der antiken Philosophie (History of Ancient Philosophy), Tübingen 1921.

KĀLĪCARAṆA : v. Avalon.

KEPLER : Judicium de Trigono igneo, ed. Frisch I, 1603.

KNAPP, Dr. Martin : Pentagramma Veneris, Basel 1934.

KUGLER, F. X. : Sternkunde und Sterndienst in Babel, Vol 2, part 2, number 2.

LOENEN, J. H. M. M. : Parmenides, Melissus, Gorgias — a Reinterpretation of Eleatic Philosophy, Assen 1959.

MELISSOS : Fragments 7/7.

NESTLE, W. : Die Vorsokratiker, Stuttgart 1956.

PEUCKERT, Will-Erich : Astrologie, Stuttgart 1960.

PTOLEMÄUS : Tetrabiblos, Loeb Classical Library, London, Cambridge, Greek-English edition of Ptolemy's work by F. E. Robbins (London/Cambridge, Mass. 1956).

REINHARDT : Parmenides und die Geschichte der griechischen Philosophie (1916) (Parmenides and the history of Greek Philosophy).

REMPLEIN, H. : Psychologie der Persönlichkeit (Psychology of Personality), Munich/Basle 1963.

ŚAṄKARĀCĀRYA : v. Brown.

SCHWABE, Julius : Archetyp und Tierkreis (Archetype and Zodiac), Basle 1951.

de SOPPER, A. J. : Wat is philosophie ? Haarlem 1954.

STERN, William : Allgemeine Psychologie auf personalistischer Grundlage (General Psychology on the foundations of personality), Den Haag 1950 'About the Temporal Perception'.

THIBAUT, G. : Astronomie, Astrologie und Mathematik, Berlin 1899.

VIVEKANANDA : Raja-Yoga, Zürich 1963, now : Hermann Bauer Verlag, Freiburg.

WELLEK, Albert : Ganzheitspsychologie und Strukturtheorie (Holistic Psychologie and Structure Theory), Bern 1955.

WERNER, Heinz : Comparative Psychology of Mental Development, New York, Chicago, Los Angeles 1948.

—— : Einführung in die Entwicklungspsychologie (Introduction to developmental psychology, Munich 1959.

WILHELM, Richard : Das Geheimnis der goldenen Blüte (The secret of the golden blossom), Zürich 1957.

ZEHREN, Erich : Das Testament der Sterne (The Testament of the stars) Berlin-Grunewald 1957.

INDEX